"I'm not stalking you, if that's what you're thinking," he said, coming toward her with that charming smile.

She couldn't help but laugh. "Well, that's a good thing because—" He cut her off before she could finish her sentence and her thought.

"I just wanted to make sure you got home safely, and…"

"And what?" she asked as he trailed off.

He moved closer and wrapped his arms around her waist. "And I wanted to kiss you good-night."

Simona's pulse spiked. Without waiting for a response, he bent and covered her lips with his. The moment their mouths met, heat flared out in every part of her body. He tangled his tongue with hers unhurriedly, as if he had all night. Her body trembled, and she moaned softly. At length, he lifted his head.

He pressed his lips to hers once more and then whispered, "Good night, Simona." Releasing her, he turned and sauntered back down the driveway.

Simona slumped against her car, heart pounding and legs shaking. She closed her eyes and tried to steady her breathing. When she opened them, he was leaning against his car. "Donovan?"

"I'm just waiting for you to go inside."

Such a gentleman. This man was breaking down her resolve.

Dear Reader,

You met Donovan Wright in my first novel, *Just to Be with You*. He had a plethora of advice on love for his best friend. Now that it's his turn, he's finding that the answers aren't so black-and-white and the hurt he's buried is not so easy to dismiss. Simona Andrews is just the woman he needs to help him move past the pain. He'll provide the unconditional love Simona has always craved. In return, she can give Donovan the one thing he wants—a family—even if he doesn't know it yet. Throw in a sweet baby girl, and poor Donovan doesn't stand a chance!

It was an absolute joy to watch Donovan fall in love. I hope you enjoy the ride, and catching up on the lives of his friends, as much as I did.

Coming up, I'm excited to bring you a new family series—the Grays. Stay tuned for details.

I love hearing from readers. Please feel free to contact me anytime.

Much love,

Sheryl

Website: SherylLister.com

Email: sheryllister@gmail.com

Facebook: Author Sheryl Lister

It's ONLY You

SHERYL LISTER

HARLEQUIN® KIMANI™ ROMANCE

Recycling programs
for this product may
not exist in your area.

ISBN-13: 978-0-373-86419-5

It's Only You

HARLEQUIN®

www.Harlequin.com

Printed in U.S.A.

Sheryl Lister has enjoyed reading and writing for as long as she can remember. When she's not reading, writing or playing chauffeur, Sheryl can be found on a date with her husband or in the kitchen creating appetizers and bite-size desserts. She holds a BS in occupational therapy and post-professional MS in occupational therapy from San Jose State University. She resides in California and is a wife, mother of three and pediatric occupational therapist.

Books by Sheryl Lister

Harlequin Kimani Romance

Just to Be with You
All of Me
It's Only You

Visit the Author Profile page at Harlequin.com for more titles.

To my amazing husband, Lance,
for your unconditional love and your unwavering support.
It's only you who sets my soul on fire.

ACKNOWLEDGMENTS

My Heavenly Father, I am nothing without You.

Thank you to my children, family and friends for
your continued support. I appreciate and love you!

A special thank-you to LaShaunda Hoffman
for your expertise and encouragement.
You've helped me more than you know.

Thank you to my editor, Rachel Burkot,
and the Harlequin Kimani team
for your editorial guidance and support.

A very special thank-you to my agent, Sarah E. Younger.
I appreciate you more than words can say.

Chapter 1

"Simona, Dr. Harris has been looking for you."

Simona Andrews barely held back an eye roll. She had been on her feet for ten hours in the hospital's emergency room and was too tired to deal with Dr. Harris's antics tonight. "Why? There are several other nurses on duty."

"True, but you're the only one on tonight with pediatric experience," the other nurse answered.

"Where is he?"

"Exam room four."

"Thanks," Simona called over her shoulder, increasing her pace. She hoped the good doctor really had a patient this time. Then she heard the crying—well, screaming, actually—from two doors away.

"Thank God," Dr. Harris muttered when he looked up and saw her enter. "Ms. Andrews, Thomas here is a victim of little brother syndrome."

He placed a subtle hand on her back, and she immediately moved out of his reach. "Hi, Thomas."

The doctor quickly explained that the child's mother had brought the two-year-old into the hospital's emergency room when he wouldn't stop crying and couldn't move his right arm. Further questioning revealed that the woman's teenage son had been swinging Thomas around in circles by his wrists, resulting in Thomas's right shoulder dislocating.

Simona moved closer to the table where Thomas sat crying, shaking his head and clinging to his mother. She knew the doctor could easily maneuver the joint back into place, but not without some pain to the child. She produced a small stuffed tiger from her pocket and extended it to him. He stared at it for a lengthy moment, then reached out to touch it. Gradually, his tears stopped.

"Does your arm hurt?" she asked softly.

He nodded, and his lip began quivering again.

She pointed to the tiger. "That's why I brought you my special friend. I think his name is the same as yours— Thomas the Tiger—and he helps little boys be brave when they get hurt. Would you like to hold him?"

He looked down at the tiger and back up at her, as if trying to decide whether Simona was telling the truth. Finally he nodded again and took it from her outstretched hand.

Simona smiled. "Now, Dr. Harris is going to fix your arm, but it might hurt a little, so Thomas the Tiger is going to stay right in your arms to help you be brave. Is that okay?"

He glanced at the doctor, back to Simona and then laid his head against his mother.

She caught the doctor's eye, and he maneuvered closer to the little boy's injured shoulder. While she told Thomas stories of the tiger's adventures with other little children, Dr. Harris worked quickly. Thomas winced and let out a small whimper, but by then the doctor had finished and stepped back.

"Wow, Thomas. You did a great job," Simona praised. "You didn't even cry."

He gave her a shy smile.

"You're such a big boy," his mother said, kissing his forehead. "Thank you, doctor."

"No problem, Mrs. Peters." He gave her some precautions and patted Thomas on the knee.

"And thank you, Ms. Andrews. I don't think my baby would've let the doctor touch him if you hadn't been here. You even calmed me down," Mrs. Peters added with a chuckle.

Simona smiled and gently stroked Thomas's back. "You're welcome. Take care, Thomas, and no more human airplanes." He reached for Simona, catching her off guard, and she hugged the toddler.

His mother stared. "I can't believe it. He never goes to strangers. You must be a baby whisperer, Ms. Andrews."

"I've said the same thing," Dr. Harris murmured.

Ignoring the doctor, she laughed. "I don't know about that, Mrs. Peters, but I love children."

"Do you have any children of your own?"

"No. But I'm a proud aunt."

"Well, you're going to make a terrific mother someday."

"I couldn't agree more," the doctor chimed in with a gleam in his eyes that went well beyond professional.

She sent a warning look his way, then turned back. "Thank you, Mrs. Peters. Let me show you to the discharge area."

Dr. Harris chuckled. "Have a good evening, Mrs. Peters, and take care, Thomas."

Glaring at him over her shoulder, Simona ushered Mrs. Peters out before she could ask any more personal questions.

"Is my son going to be okay?" the woman asked nervously as they walked out.

She smiled reassuringly. "Your son will be fine, Mrs. Peters, but please make sure you tell your other children not to swing Thomas by his arms. As the doctor said, at this age his joints have not completely developed, and it's easy for them to slip out."

"Thank you, I will. Believe me, if I see one of them so much as tug on Thomas's arm, *they're* going to be the ones in the emergency room." She shook her head. "I've told them over and over to quit swinging him around. Wait until I get home," she fussed. She cradled Thomas against her shoulder and stroked his back lovingly while avoiding his injured side.

After leaving the woman with the discharge clerk, Simona headed back to the nurses' station, still seething. Doctor Lionel Harris had been coming on to her since she had started working at the hospital, taking every opportunity to make suggestive comments. He had even gone so far as to lure her into an empty treatment room under the guise of needing assistance with a patient.

At thirty-six, he had been featured on the covers of several magazines and was a sought-after lecturer for his knowledge of emergency medicine. Combined with his charm and good looks, he'd be the perfect guy for some woman—just not her. But for some reason, he couldn't take no for an answer.

Simona had relocated to Los Angeles from Oakland a year ago to escape the drama that had become her life, and she had no desire to hook up with someone as famous as Dr. Harris and have her relationship play out for all to see. And that would be exactly what would happen if she—a nurse—started dating one of the most attractive doctors on staff. Had it not been for her grandmother, she might have moved clear across the country after breaking up with her ex. LA was close enough to Nana, but big enough to get lost in. Now she only wanted to do her job and go home—no drama and no men.

"Hey, Simona. What are you doing here? I thought you were off at seven."

"Hey, Phyllis. I was supposed to be, but Annette called in sick and Dr. Cortez asked if I'd cover the first four hours. Betty is covering the rest of the shift. Then I'm off until Tuesday morning."

Phyllis nodded. "Lucky you. One hour to go. Right before all the heavy weekend drama starts."

The weekends were always busy in the emergency room—more parties and drinking often translated to more fights and accidents. Simona was glad to be off.

Another nurse rushed over to them and clutched Simona's arm. "Oh, my God!" she whispered excitedly. "You're never going to guess who's here in the hospital."

"Who?" Phyllis asked.

"*Monte*. I think his wife is having a baby. He is sooo fine, and his music…" She sighed dreamily.

Simona stared at the young nurse, whose name she couldn't remember, and shook her head. She'd heard of the popular R & B singer and producer, and owned a few of his CDs, but had no idea he had a wife or that she was expecting a baby.

"We should go up and see if we can get his autograph. I have all his CDs."

Simona glanced down at the woman's badge. "No, we shouldn't, Alyssa," she said firmly. "What we *should* do is allow the man to have some privacy. This is a hospital, not a concert venue. How about displaying a little professionalism?" People not respecting other's privacy topped the list of Simona's pet peeves.

Alyssa had the decency to look embarrassed…for about five seconds. "It's just a little autograph. Geez, lighten up."

Simona was poised to give Alyssa a blistering retort, but

the sound of sirens interrupted whatever she had planned to say. She and Phyllis shared a look and rushed off with Alyssa trailing them.

Donovan Wright pushed through the hospital doors and went to the front desk. "Can you tell me what floor maternity is on?"

"Fourth," the older woman behind the desk answered with a smile. "Is this your first?"

His heart clenched. "It's not mine. I'm here for a friend."

"Oh. I just thought…well, a handsome guy like you should have no problem finding a wife."

He smiled, thanked her, then sauntered off toward the elevators, his loafers echoing loudly on the highly polished floors.

As he waited for the elevator, he pondered the woman's statement. No problem finding a wife? *Yeah. Right.* Donovan stepped in when the doors opened, pushed the button for the fourth floor and leaned his head back against the wall.

Closing his eyes, he exhaled deeply. He was exhausted. With Terrence out of the office for the past week, Donovan had been working sixteen-hour days at the record company just to keep up. As the executive vice president of RC Productions he oversaw most of the departments and had managed the music career of Terrence—who used the stage name Monte—for the past decade, along with one other group at the record label.

He'd been up to his eyeballs scheduling tour dates, negotiating fees, going over contracts and meeting with various entities. If not for his two assistants, he would more than likely still be sitting at his desk despite the fact that it was nine thirty.

Two years ago, both he and Terrence had worked long hours at the record company Terrence started. With Terrence taking on the role of CEO and producer and working on his own music, they'd had no choice. But since Terrence and Janae married, his friend made a point of not staying late as often as he used to. Now, with the new baby, Donovan wondered if Terrence would be working even less and if they would need to hire another executive just to keep up.

The elevator doors opened on the fourth floor, and he followed the signs to the nurses' station. Before he could ask, Donovan spotted Terrence and met him halfway. He brought Terrence in for a one-armed hug.

"What's up, man? The baby here yet?"

"Hey, D. Not yet," Terrence answered.

"You look exhausted. How's Janae holding up?"

"It's been over eight hours, and I know she's in a lot of pain, but she refuses to take anything. She wants to do this naturally." He scrubbed a hand over his head. "I feel so helpless."

Donovan clapped him on the shoulder. "Well, hopefully it won't be much longer. What are the doctors saying?"

"They just checked her and said she's eight centimeters dilated, so I'm praying it won't be much longer. I was on my way to the waiting room to tell my grandparents before I go back in."

"They're here?" Donovan asked, following Terrence.

"You know they'll be here all night, if necessary. They're more excited than we are."

Donovan laughed. "I can imagine."

Terrence's grandparents had been his only family until he married Janae. Both were in their seventies, but rose swiftly when the two men entered.

"Is my great-grandbaby here yet?" Terrence's grandmother asked.

"Not yet, Grandma." He told her the same thing he'd told Donovan.

"Hi, Donovan. I didn't expect to see you here tonight. Terrence told me about all the late hours you've been working."

"Hey, Grandma. You know I had to be here for the birth of my first godchild." Donovan leaned down to kiss her cheek. He extended his hand to Terrence's grandfather. "How's it going, Mr. Campbell?"

"Can't complain."

"I need to get back," Terrence said.

"I'll wait here with your grandparents, T. Give Janae my best."

"I will," he called over his shoulder, hurrying off.

Donovan sprawled out on a loveseat, dangling his legs over the armrest. He spent a few minutes catching up with the grandparents, then asked, "How long have you two been here?"

"About four hours," Mr. Campbell answered.

"Let's hope it won't be much longer," Grandma said. "I'm so glad Terrence found someone to share his life with. You know, Donovan, if my stubborn, commitment-phobic grandson can find a wife, I'm certain you can, too," she added casually.

Uh-oh. "I've been too busy to even think about a relationship."

"Well, no time like the present to slow down and smell a few roses. Don't you think? What happened to the young lady you were seeing a while back? She came with you to one or two of the barbecues. The two of you seemed quite serious, and I thought for sure there'd be wedding bells in your future."

Donovan leaned back, closed his eyes and frowned at the mention of his ex-girlfriend. Rolanda Evans had committed what he considered an unpardonable sin—she'd betrayed his trust in so many ways. In his mind, no trust equaled no relationship. "We broke up a long time ago."

"Hmm, so you haven't found someone else?"

"No, ma'am." And he hadn't been looking. He sincerely prayed this birth wouldn't take long. Miss Ellie was worse than his mother. Since his mother lived far from LA, he could dodge her easily. Not so much with Terrence's grandmother. However, now that his small circle of friends had all married, lately he was starting to feel like a fifth wheel.

"Ellie, quit badgering the boy," Mr. Campbell said with a chuckle.

She shrugged. "He calls me Grandma, and that gives me privileges."

Had he known Eleanor Campbell's sweet offer to call her Grandma came with *privileges*, he would have refused it in a heartbeat and run in the opposite direction. Maybe it wasn't too late to go back to Mrs. Campbell or Miss Ellie.

"One of the ladies in my yoga class mentioned that her great-niece had just moved to the city. I saw a picture, and she's absolutely gorgeous. I think she's around thirty—"

Donovan sat up abruptly, swung his legs around and jumped up. "Um, Miss Ellie…"

She laughed. "So, we're back to Miss Ellie, huh? All right. I'll leave you alone for now." Miss Ellie pointed a finger his way. "But you need a wife."

Before he could form a response, Terrence burst through the door.

"We have a baby girl," Terrence announced with tears in his eyes. "A beautiful five-pound three-ounce baby girl."

"Oh, my," Miss Ellie cried.

"Congratulations, son." Mr. Campbell engulfed Terrence in a bear hug.

"Congratulations, T," Donovan added. "How are mom and baby?"

"Janae is understandably exhausted, but she's good. They're checking the baby now. Since she's almost a month early, they want to be sure nothing is wrong. But my girl has a set of lungs already. I think she's gonna sing with her daddy," Terrence said proudly. "Let me get back. I'll come get you guys in a little while."

Forty-five minutes later, Terrence escorted the trio to Janae's room. Donovan hung back to allow Terrence's grandparents some time with their new great-granddaughter.

"Donovan, come meet your goddaughter," Janae said.

He approached the bed, leaned down and placed a kiss on Janae's cheek. "Congratulations, Mama. She's a beauty. Thank goodness she takes after you and not Terrence," he joked.

They all laughed, and Terrence said, "Don't mess around and get your godfather card revoked in the first hour."

Janae handed him the baby. "Say hello to Nadia Elise Campbell."

Donovan gently cradled the tiny bundle against his chest. He placed a soft kiss on her forehead.

"Hey, Nadia. I'm your Uncle Donovan. You and I are going to have so much fun together." He dug his cell out of his pocket and handed it to Terrence. "Get a shot of me with my little goddaughter. Oh, and take a couple extras. You know Mrs. Lewis will have my head if I show up Monday morning without pictures." Mrs. Lewis was Terrence's secretary, and the older woman loved Terrence like a son.

"No lie." Terrence laughed, snapped a few pictures and handed the phone back.

Donovan pocketed the phone and adjusted the baby in his arms. She opened her eyes, stretched and then closed her eyes again. Emotions unlike anything he had ever felt engulfed him, and he couldn't stop staring at the petite baby with a head full of dark curls framing her small face.

"You okay, D?" Terrence asked.

Donovan blinked back the tears clouding his vision,

lifted his head and met Terrence's scrutinizing gaze. "Yeah, man." He transferred Nadia to her father.

"We've known each other a long time, and I know something's up. This isn't the first time I've noticed it," he whispered.

Donovan ignored the comment. "Does Karen know Nadia came a little early?"

Terrence raised a brow, but didn't press. "No. She and Damian are finally taking their honeymoon cruise." Karen was Janae's best friend. She'd gotten married several months earlier, but due to her job as an elementary school principal they'd postponed the honeymoon until after the school year ended.

Donovan took a quick peek at his watch. "It's after eleven o'clock. I need to get out of here. I have an early morning telephone conference."

"Is everything okay?"

"Fine. You just concentrate on your family. We'll take care of the office."

"I know. Thanks, man. I'll call you."

Donovan said his goodbyes, trekked back to the elevator and rode the four floors down. He rounded the corner and crossed the lobby, noting that the front desk was now empty. As he reached the entrance, he saw a sign indicating he would have to exit through Emergency. Changing directions, he shoved his hands in his pockets and started toward the other exit.

His mind went back to his goddaughter. He hadn't expected the riot of emotions that swirled in his gut when he held Nadia. As hard as he tried to keep the distant memories from surfacing, they came anyway. He inhaled deeply and forced them down. Out of the corner of his eye, movement caught his attention, interrupting his thoughts. Then he heard a woman's startled cry. Donovan took off at a dead run.

He caught the falling woman around the waist with one arm and helped the other person steady the tumbling coffee cart with his free hand. He registered the searing pain as his arm snagged the edge of the cart, and hot coffee spilled over his forearm.

"Oh, my goodness! I'm so sorry." The young woman pushing the cart snatched up the remaining carafes, trying to keep them from falling to the floor with the other two.

Donovan jerked his arm back and grimaced. "It's okay."

She rushed off and pushed through the door into what he assumed was the ladies' room.

He turned to the woman in his embrace. "Are you all right?"

She nodded, but her trembling body told a different story. He instinctively pulled her closer. "It's okay. You're safe now." She released a deep sigh and moved closer, burying her head in his chest. The way she clung to him stirred something deep inside him. *I was just keeping her from being knocked down,* he quickly told himself.

"I guess I wasn't watching where I was going," she finally said.

Adrenaline still pumped through his veins, his heart hadn't returned to a normal pace and the pain in his arm was increasing. Yet none of it erased the strange feelings evoked by holding this woman in his arms.

Pushing them aside, he rationalized that they were probably due to the excitement of the evening—the birth of his first godchild—and pure exhaustion.

Nothing more.

Chapter 2

Simona tried to steady her emotions. She had been so deep in thought that she hadn't even heard the cart approaching. The collision had nearly given her a heart attack. Slowly she wrapped her arms around the man's waist. "Thank…thank you."

He tightened his arms around her and caressed her back. "Anytime. Are you sure you're okay?"

Her heart continued to race from being scared out of her wits and, even more alarming, from the overwhelming sense of security she gained from being in her rescuer's arms.

She heard footsteps behind them and glanced around his shoulder to see the volunteer returning with a wad of paper towels and one of the hospital's security officers close behind.

"Ms. Andrews, are you okay?" the security guard asked, narrowing his gaze at the man holding Simona.

She lifted her head and stepped out of the man's embrace, rubbing her hip where the cart had hit her. "Yes. Thanks to him." She glanced up to find her rescuer watching her intently, concern etched in his features. She immediately moved her hand away from her hip.

"What happened?"

Tearing her gaze away from his intense stare, she turned toward the guard. "Um…just a little accident. I wasn't paying attention and didn't see the cart." Simona glanced down at the hospital volunteer trying to mop up the mess. "Maybe you should call maintenance to clean that up."

"Yeah, probably," the woman mumbled, clearly embarrassed.

The guard asked, "Are you hurt?"

Simona shook her head. "I'm okay."

"Are you sure? There's blood on your top."

She looked down at her top, held it out and frowned. "I don't know how…" She shifted her gaze to the man standing next to her. "Oh, my goodness! You're bleeding."

He tried to wave her off, but she moved in front of him, lifted his arm and examined the wound below his rolled-up shirtsleeve, which was stained with coffee. "I'm fine."

"No, you're not. You've got a nasty cut and a burn. I need to get you inside to emergency."

"Really. It's just a little cut," he protested, withdrawing his arm. "Nothing that requires a three-hour wait in emergency."

Simona reached for his uninjured arm and pulled him in the direction of the emergency room, leaving the guard to deal with the cleanup.

As soon as they got to the entrance, his steps slowed. "You're wearing scrubs. Are you a doctor?"

"No. An emergency room nurse." She led him past a half-full waiting room to the back.

"Simona, what are you still doing here? I thought you were off," a nurse said as they entered a treatment room.

"I am. Is there a doctor available? I think he's going to need stitches." Simona usually assisted the doctor with the minor procedure, but with the way her hands were shaking she'd probably do more harm than good.

"I'll go find somebody." The woman hurried off.

"Have a seat, and let's see if I can get this bleeding to stop. Then I'll clean it up and put something on this burn."

He sat on the examination table. "I still don't think you need to go through all this trouble." He caught her hand as she took a step. "I'm more concerned about you. Are you sure you're okay? Maybe we should have the doctor check you out. After all, you did almost lose your life to a coffee cart, and I noticed you rubbing your hip."

She gasped softly. His gentle touch and soothing, deep voice sent a wave of heat through her body. Simona lifted her head and couldn't stop staring at him. In the hall, she had been too distracted to focus on his features, but he was easily the most handsome man she had ever laid eyes on. His clean-shaven walnut-colored face, close-cropped hair and light brown eyes nearly took her breath away, tempting her to reach up and run her hands across the smooth, defined planes. She shook off the dangerous thought, reminding herself to behave like a professional. "Really, I'm fine, Mister…um…I'm sorry, what's your name?"

He held her eyes intently. "Donovan. Donovan Wright. And you?"

"Simona Andrews."

"It's a pleasure to meet you, Simona."

Her name flowed from his lips like a gentle caress, and her pulse skipped when his mouth inched up in a sexy smile, revealing a dimple in his left cheek. *Focus, Simona!* "I'm so sorry you got hurt, and…and look at your shirt. It's ruined. I'll replace it."

"Don't worry about it."

He lifted his arm at the same time as she reached for his

sleeve and their hands touched again, inflaming her senses
once more. She withdrew quickly, turned and grabbed a
pair of gloves from the box on the wall. The gloves might
protect her from any potential diseases, but not from the
awareness flowing between her and this man.

She inspected the burn. There was redness and swelling.
Simona noticed the bleeding had slowed from the cut, but
handed him some gauze to apply pressure to the wound
and put an ice pack on the burn. She pulled the computer
stand over to take a medical history. He was thirty-five
years old, six feet two inches tall, and weighed one eighty-
five. Recalling his agility and strength when he kept her
from falling, and how his hard body felt pressed against
hers, she could add that he was in excellent shape.

The doctor arrived shortly after, donned a pair of gloves
and introduced himself as Dr. Cortez. "Mr. Wright, can
you please remove your arm from the sleeve?" He examined the cut and determined that Donovan's wound re-
quired stitches. Then he checked the burn. "I don't think
the burn is going to blister."

Simona stood transfixed by the sculpted muscles in
Donovan's arm and chest. Their eyes met, and he smiled
knowingly. Simona turned away and busied herself with
assisting the doctor.

"What are you still doing here, Ms. Andrews?" Dr. Cortez asked as he applied a local anesthetic.

She told him what happened in the hallway.

"Were you hurt?"

"No. I'm fine, thanks to Mr. Wright."

"Mr. Wright, I'm very grateful you were here."

"So am I," Mr. Wright murmured, angling his head
her way.

Pretending to be busy, she refused to meet his gaze
directly.

Gathering his supplies, Dr. Cortez worked quickly.

Once the wound was closed and covered with a large gauze bandage, the doctor applied an ointment to the burn then stripped off his gloves. "You'll need to keep that dry for the next forty-eight hours and have the stitches removed in ten days. I'll give you a prescription for the ointment. Apply it three times a day. When was your last tetanus shot?"

"I don't remember. It's been a while."

"More than ten years?" When Donovan nodded, he said, "You'll need to get one. I'll call one of the nurses to take care of it."

"I'll do it," Simona said.

The doctor nodded. "Mr. Wright, thank you again. Consider your bill paid in full."

"Thanks, Dr. Cortez."

After the doctor left, they stared at each other in silence. Simona was so busy gawking that it took her a moment to remember she was supposed to be giving him a tetanus shot. "I'll be right back."

"Okay."

As soon as she stepped out of the room, two nurses rushed over and asked about what happened. Apparently news traveled fast. After recounting the story two more times, she said, "I really need to get back to my patient."

Before returning, she ducked into an empty room. Knowing she had only a minute, she pulled out her cell and dialed. "Hey, Eve."

"Hi, Simona. What's up? I thought you were getting off at eleven."

"I was. I can't go into it right now, but I'll be home as soon as I can."

"No problem. I'm just sitting here working on my essay. Are you okay?"

Simona blew out a long breath. "Yeah. How is she?"

"Sleeping peacefully. Everything is fine."

"You're a lifesaver, Eve. I'll see you later."

"Okay."

Simona didn't know how she would have managed over the past four weeks without her neighbor's help. She didn't easily trust, but Eve Thompson, with her direct speech and compassionate heart, had won Simona over almost immediately.

She disconnected, put the phone in her pocket and re-traced her steps to where Donovan waited, stopping first at the cabinet where medications were stored and remind-ing herself to remain professional.

Donovan sat on the examination table thinking about Simona. Earlier, his concern had been for her safety. Now, in the light and with the threat removed, he couldn't take his eyes off her. She was stunning. Braids swept up into a ponytail that gave him an unobstructed view of her coffee-with-cream complexion, wide dark brown eyes and bow-shaped lips, perfect for kissing.

He shook his head. *Damn, I must be tired.* No, if he were honest, fatigue had nothing to do with it. He was attracted to his nurse, plain and simple. He lifted his left arm, studied the dressing and shook his head. Donovan looked up when Simona entered the room with a syringe and sheet of paper on a tray.

She handed him the paper. "Here's the prescription for the ointment."

"Thanks."

"It's really late, so let's finish up and get you out of here," Simona said. "Which arm would you prefer? You might have some pain and stiffness for a couple of days, as well as some redness or swelling."

"May as well do it in the left. No sense in having both arms messed up," he said wryly.

Soft laughter escaped her lips.

The warm sound filled the room, and the shy smile

curving her mouth did something to his insides. Despite her flustered state earlier, she was now poised and in control.

She swabbed the area with alcohol and injected him. "Okay. All done. You can put your shirt back on. Do you need some help?"

"Nah, I'm fine." He carefully maneuvered his arm through the sleeve and buttoned the shirt. Coffee stained the left sleeve and down the front.

"So…um…you're free to leave now," she said, depositing the needle in a container affixed to the wall and removing her gloves.

"Aren't you off?"

She turned back to face him. "Yes."

He slid from the table. "Then, come on. I'll walk you to your car."

"You don't have to do that. I'm sure the security guards are waiting to walk me out."

A man rushed into the room before Donovan could reply. A doctor, he guessed, judging by the white coat and stethoscope hanging around his neck.

The man rushed over to Simona and placed his arm around her shoulder, which she promptly shrugged off. "Simona, I heard about what happened. Are you okay?"

"Fine, Dr. Harris. I was just leaving."

"Great. I'll walk you out."

"I got it, doc. I'm sure you need to get back to your patients," Donovan said, picking up on the obvious tension between the two. "You ready, Simona?"

"Yes. Thank you, Donovan. Good night, Dr. Harris."

The doctor looked ready to explode, and Donovan chuckled inwardly. Placing a hand on the small of her back, he guided Simona out. "Have a good evening, doctor."

Neither spoke as they made their way out of the building. A few steps outside, she slowed.

"Which way is your car?"

She gestured to the right. "I appreciate you walking me out."

"Simona, there's no way I'd let you walk out here alone. Do you normally get off work this late?" Donovan didn't see a security guard, and it more than concerned him.

"No. I get off at seven. Tonight I was covering part of another nurse's shift because she called in sick."

"So, what's the story on you and the doctor? Are you two dating or something?"

She angled her head to look up at him and paused before saying, "No, but not for lack of trying on his part."

Donovan was secretly elated by that fact.

She stopped next to a Honda Accord sedan. "Well... um...this is my car. I don't know how to thank you."

"Hey. Don't worry about it."

"And you got hurt. I'm so sorry."

"Simona, there is no reason to apologize. It was an accident."

She nodded and unlocked the door.

He reached around and opened it for her. "Do you need me to follow you home?"

"No, I'll be fine." Simona came up on tiptoe and kissed his cheek. "Thank you, Donovan...for everything. If you ever need anything, let me know." She lowered herself into the car.

The warmth of her lips against his cheek sent electricity through his body, and he fought the temptation to turn into the kiss. "Are you working tomorrow?"

"No. I'm off until Tuesday. Why?"

"Just concerned. Make sure someone walks out with you, okay?"

"It won't be dark when I get off at seven, so there shouldn't be a problem."

"Simona, promise me you won't come out alone. I wouldn't want anything to happen to you."

She stared up at him with a strange expression, then nodded.

"Thank you. Good night and take care of yourself."

She smiled. "I will. Good night."

Donovan closed her door and stepped back. He waited until she started the engine and drove off before heading across the lot to his own car. He unlocked the doors, climbed in and shut the door. Leaning his head back, he closed his eyes as a wave of fatigue hit him. It had been a long day and a crazy night. Sitting upright, he started the car, backed out and drove home.

Twenty-five minutes later, Donovan turned into his driveway and pulled into the garage. He dragged his weary body out of the car, entered the house through the side door and pressed a wall switch to close the garage door.

He tossed his keys onto the kitchen counter and reached into the refrigerator for a bottle of water. Unscrewing the cap, he took a long drink and wished it were something stronger. The mail sat piled up on one end of the island where his housekeeper placed it, but he was too tired to bother with it tonight. Instead, he trekked up the stairs to his bedroom, flipped on the nightstand lamp and dropped down on the side of the bed. *Helluva night*, he mused. He sat a moment longer, then went to shower.

It took some maneuvering, but he managed to shower, dry off and brush his teeth in a reasonable amount of time. Turning off the bathroom light and bedside lamp, he returned to his bedroom, pulled back the covers and crawled into bed. Donovan glanced over at the clock. It was nearly one in the morning, and he needed to be up and in his office by six thirty. Even though it was a Saturday, he had to take care of some tour logistics for Kaleidoscope's concert tomorrow night on the East Coast. With any luck, he could take care of everything in less than two hours and be back home and in bed by nine thirty, ten at the latest.

He moved to a more comfortable position, making sure to keep his left arm free, and closed his eyes. Donovan made a mental note to call his doctor to schedule a follow-up appointment. He was beyond exhausted, but his mind continued to race with thoughts of Simona. True, she was beautiful, but something more appealed to him—her strength and compassion, maybe. Why hadn't he asked her for her phone number?

Next time, he thought with a smile.

Chapter 3

Two seconds after Simona entered the house, Eve rushed across the room and grabbed her in a hug.

"Girl, I was worried out of my mind. It's going on one o'clock. I was about to call you again. What happened?" Eve released her and frowned.

Simona walked over to the couch and lowered her weary body down. "I was basically run over by one of the hospital volunteers pushing a coffee cart."

"Are you all right?"

"I'm okay. Just a little shaken, and bruised where the cart hit my hip."

Eve sat next to Simona. "If that's all, what took you so long to get home?"

"I had to help Donovan. He got hurt."

Eve lifted an eyebrow. "Donovan?"

"Yeah. He's the guy who came to my rescue. I feel so bad because he got cut and burned in the process."

Eve grasped her hand. "Is he hurt bad?"

Simona shook her head. "He had about a three-inch gash on his forearm that had to be stitched up, and the burn doesn't look like it'll be too bad, so he's okay, thank God. I don't know what I would've done if he'd been hurt seriously. The crazy thing is, even though he was still bleeding and in obvious pain, he was more concerned about having a doctor check me out."

"Sounds like a real-life knight in shining armor."

"He was—though I really wish he'd had the armor on," she said absently. Memories of being held in his strong arms replayed in her mind. She should have at least gotten his phone number…to make good on her offer to replace his shirt, of course. His information was in the system, so she could get it that way. But…

A touch on her hand broke into her musings.

"Simona," Eve called.

"I'm sorry. Did you say something?"

Eve smiled. "Mmm-hmm. I was asking about your knight, and you drifted off into fairy tale land. He must have been something."

Fine as all get out, rock hard body, and seemingly an all-around good guy—yep, he was something.

Eve laughed.

"What?"

"You're daydreaming again. What does he look like?"

"A little over six feet, handsome, muscles—"

"In other words, fine as *hell*."

Simona smiled and nodded. "Yes, he is." She pushed to her feet. "I'm wiped out. I need to hit the shower and go to bed. Did you have any problems tonight?"

Eve stood. "Not a one. She's an angel. Woke up an hour ago for a few minutes but went right back to sleep." She went over to the dining room table and gathered up her belongings. "I'll see you later."

Simona walked her neighbor to the door and waited

until Eve went inside her house before closing her own door. Simona picked up the monitor off the table, turned off the lights and went down the short hallway to the first bedroom. A nightlight illuminated the baby lying in her crib. Simona stood staring at her niece's small form for several minutes, the covers rising and falling in rhythm as she slept.

Yasmine had been born two months prematurely to Simona's twenty-two-year-old younger sister—her namesake—who had died in childbirth as a result of injuries she'd sustained in a car accident. Although they were able to save the baby, her sister and her sister's fiancé hadn't been as fortunate. Simona still couldn't believe that her sister was gone, but her niece reminded her of that fact daily. Yasmine had spent six weeks in the NICU after birth and was on a ventilator for the first two. So far, there hadn't been any more problems, but Simona kept a close watch on her.

Simona's grandmother had wanted to raise Yasmine, but taking care of a small baby was too much for Nana, so Simona had driven to Oakland two months ago and brought the baby back to LA. Fortunately, after Simona explained her dilemma, Mrs. Battle, the charge nurse, allowed her to change her schedule to four eight-hour days a week.

Simona stood a few minutes longer, smiling at the miniature version of her sister as sadness rose up once again. Seven years Yasmine's senior, Simona had been close with her baby sister, and she missed Yasmine's infectious laughter and zeal for life. Looking down at her sleeping niece, Simona vowed to raise the little girl with all the love in her heart, just as Yasmine would have done. She leaned down and brushed a soft kiss on her eleven-month-old niece's forehead, checked the baby monitor to make sure it was on and continued to her bedroom.

Thirty minutes later, freshly showered, Simona pulled

back the bed covers, laid her worn-out body down and groaned. She was exhausted, and with any luck, she'd be able to get a few hours of sleep before Yasmine woke up.

Automatically, her mind went back to Donovan. His hands on her had created sensations she hadn't felt in a long time, and she wished she could have stayed in his arms all night. Her eyes snapped open. Where had that thought come from? She'd spent the past year purposely staying away from men, and now she lay fantasizing about one.

"You're just exhausted, Simona," she mumbled to herself. Given the circumstances, it was natural to have these types of feelings, she assured herself. She closed her eyes again, but Donovan's handsome face wouldn't leave her. It took a while, but she finally drifted off.

Time seemed to accelerate, and before she knew it, Simona was walking across the hospital parking lot Tuesday to start her shift. Dealing with the fast pace of an emergency room at only twenty-nine, Simona thought she had good endurance. But adjusting to Yasmine's routine and working four days a week was proving to be more of a challenge than she'd envisioned.

The first few hours went by in a blur, and she was more than ready to sit for a minute when her lunch break came around. Yet no matter how tired she felt, somehow Donovan always worked his way into her psyche. Would she ever see him again? She told herself she only wanted to see him to make sure he was okay, but knew she lied. His concern for her well-being had gone far beyond the call of duty and was truly touching. While eating, her thoughts strayed to Donovan. Again. As much as she wanted to call him, she didn't feel right about getting his information from the hospital records. So she would have to be content with the memory of her knight.

* * *

"Thanks. I'll have the contract out to you by the beginning of next week." Donovan hung up, finished making notes on the contract sheet and called in his secretary. It was only Tuesday, and the week promised to be a long one.

"Yes, Donovan."

He glanced up from the papers. "Monique, I just confirmed the two dates for Monte at the Catalina Island JazzTrax Festival in October and the Nokia Theater in November." He handed her the papers. "Can you type up the contracts and have them ready for Brad by tomorrow?"

She accepted the sheets and handed him a telephone message. "Sure. Mrs. Lake from the Artistic Inspirations Foundation called again. She wanted to confirm whether Monte would still be conducting the vocal and piano workshops at the upcoming art camp. I told her we'd call her back because I didn't know if he'd be available since the baby came early."

The nonprofit foundation worked tirelessly to promote the importance of music and the arts in schools and the community. Thanks to generous donations, every summer they hosted a two-week day camp for students in grades four through twelve to experience the arts. At the end of the two weeks, the foundation put on an art show and concert.

"Okay. I'll check with him and call her back. Thanks."

"If you don't need anything else, I'm going to head out."

He glanced up at the wall clock to see it was already past five. "No. Have a good evening."

"You, too. See you in the morning."

Donovan followed her out to the hallway but went in the opposite direction, toward Terrence's office. He found Terrence's secretary standing at the file cabinet. "Hey, Mrs. Lewis. I'm sorry I didn't get over here sooner."

"Oh, don't worry about it. I know you've got your hands full. Have you talked to Monte today?"

"No. I haven't talked to him since last Friday at the hospital." He'd hit the ground running yesterday and barely had time to show her the pictures of Nadia.

"Well, I know you'll be dropping by his home sometime this week, so can you take this with you?" She rounded her desk, pulled an envelope from a drawer and handed it to him. "Tell him and Janae I said congratulations."

"Okay. Is there anything I need to know or anything that has come up?"

"Audrey stopped by earlier and took care of a few things, but other than that, no."

He nodded. "I won't keep you, then. See you—"

"What happened to your arm?" she asked, cutting him off.

Donovan followed her gaze to his left arm. He had forgotten that he'd rolled his sleeves up. "Oh, it's nothing."

She frowned. "Donovan Wright, *nothing* wouldn't require stitches." She planted her hands on her hips and glared at him, waiting.

Her tone, as well as the accompanying look, had him spilling his guts about the incident in the hospital hallway.

"Oh, my word! You were lucky. Burns can be nasty. Is the young lady all right?"

"I noticed her rubbing her hip where the cart hit her, but she said she was fine."

"Thank goodness. I know she's grateful you were there. Have you checked on her since then?"

He hadn't and wanted to kick himself for not getting her phone number. "No, but I will. I know it's quitting time for you. I'll walk you out," he said, changing the subject.

She smiled. "Your parents raised such a nice young man. I know they're proud of you."

He chuckled. "Thanks. I'll remind them of that the next

time I talk to them. They'll be glad to know all their hard work didn't go to waste."

Donovan walked Mrs. Lewis to her car, then came back upstairs to call Terrence.

"What's up, D?" Terrence said when he answered.

"Hey. How's the family?"

"My girls are good. Sometimes I still can't believe it. I just want to hold Nadia all day, but Janae makes me put her down," he grumbled.

He chuckled. "I take it she's spoiled already."

"I can't help it. She grabbed my heart the moment she was born."

A flash of memories crossed Donovan's mind. "Mine, too," he murmured. "Anyway, the reason I'm calling is Mrs. Lake wants to know if you're still going to donate your time to the foundation's art camp this year. It's the first two weeks in August, three weeks away."

"Definitely. I love doing the camp. Janae's parents will be here, and Karen and Damian are planning to come down, as well. We'll probably do a little barbecue or something the first weekend in August, so don't plan anything. There's nothing on the calendar, is there?"

"Other than Sheila's concert in two weeks, no. August will be a little less busy, and I'm having Joy and Nigel travel with Kaleidoscope."

"Good. By the way, you should bring a date to the barbecue. My grandmother mentioned trying to fix you up with the niece of one of her yoga classmates."

Donovan groaned. "Aw, man. I know. She's worse than my mom."

Terrence laughed. "I tried to warn you about calling her Grandma, but you wouldn't listen. So should I invite the woman?"

"Hell, no. I can get my own date. Besides, you're the last person who needs to be giving anybody dating advice.

If I recall correctly, I'm the one who helped you when you almost lost Janae."

"Yeah," he said quietly. "I owe you, man. Janae is my life."

"I know. Tell Janae hello, and kiss my goddaughter for me. I'll be by tomorrow or the next day."

"I will. Later."

Donovan disconnected and leaned back in his chair. Once again, memories of his failed relationship filled his head. He'd immersed himself in work to bury the hurt. But seeing how happy Terrence was had him contemplating trying again. Simona's face floated through his mind. He glanced up at the clock and made the decision to be there when she got off work in forty-five minutes. He stood, packed up and headed to the parking garage.

The normally thirty-minute drive took almost an hour due to traffic, and by the time he parked and strode across the hospital lot he was hoping he hadn't missed her.

A woman looked up as he approached the emergency room front desk. "Hello." She held out a clipboard. "Just fill out the information and bring it up when you're finished. We'll get you back as soon as we can."

"I'm not here to be seen. I was looking for Simona Andrews."

Her brow lifted. "Simona?"

"Yes. She's a nurse. Is she still here?"

The woman gave him the once-over then picked up the phone. She spoke quietly into the headset, nodded and hung up. "She's still here. Have a seat, and she'll be out shortly."

"Thank you." Donovan took a chair across the room. There were only a few people in the waiting area—a mother pacing while holding a small baby, an elderly couple and a man holding an ice pack against his face.

He picked up a sports magazine off the table and flipped through it.

Some time later, the doors swung open and he saw Simona searching the room. Their eyes locked, and hers widened for a second before her brows knit in confusion. He tossed the magazine on the table, stood and walked to meet her halfway.

"Donovan," she said with surprise. "Are you okay? Is something wrong with your arm?"

"No, there's nothing wrong, Simona. It's healing nicely."

"Oh. Then why are you here?"

"I wanted to check on you, to make sure you were okay."

"That's really sweet of you, but I'm fine."

"Good. Are you still getting off now?"

"Yes."

"Would you like to go out to dinner?"

"Dinner?"

"Yeah. You know, that meal that usually follows lunch."

She smiled. "I know what dinner is, Mr. Wright."

"So…yes, no?"

"Well, I…um…I…"

He leaned closer. "You did say to let you know if I needed anything, remember?"

"I remember, but this sounds a bit like blackmail," Simona said with a laugh.

Donovan shrugged. "Hey, a man's gotta do what a man's gotta do sometimes. And if it gets you to say yes to dinner, then it's all good. Well…" he hedged.

She seemed to consider his offer for a moment, then nodded. "All right, but we can't go anywhere fancy. I don't have anything except these scrubs."

"No problem. You can choose the place." He was just glad she had agreed.

"I'll be back in a few minutes." She turned and went back through the doors.

"Take your time." He stared after her and couldn't stop the smile curving his mouth. Although she was cautious, he sensed a spark there.

Donovan planned to discover everything he could about Simona Andrews, and if he had anything to say about it, tonight's date would be the first of many.

Chapter 4

Simona paced the staff break room, not sure she had done the right thing by accepting Donovan's dinner offer. Sure, she told herself, she wanted to see him again, but it wasn't something she was ready for tonight. Hadn't she promised herself not to get caught up with another man who could disrupt her quiet life?

She also had Yasmine to think about now and had no intention of bringing a string of men around her young niece. Besides, most men would run screaming at the mention of a child. But Donovan's smile and easygoing manner made it hard to say no. And, as much as she didn't want to admit it, she was glad to see him. Sighing, she pulled out her cell.

"Hey, Eve," Simona said when Eve answered.

"Hey, girl. You have to work late again?"

"No. Donovan showed up and invited me to dinner. But if you have to leave, I'll just tell him no," she quickly added.

Eve chuckled. "So, your knight is back, huh? Go, girl!

Yasmine and I are just fine. It's about time for you to get your groove back."

"Look who's talking. I don't see you going out with any guys."

"That's because I'm still basking in my singleness. After giving seven years to my jerk of an ex-husband, I need time to do all those things the cheating bastard was doing with his mistress. His money and my classes keep me quite busy."

Simona laughed.

"But you don't have an excuse, so have a great time at dinner. Let your hair down and have some fun. Bye." She hung up before Simona could respond.

Smiling, she shook her head and pocketed the phone. Walking over to the mirror, she released her long braids from the elastic band and redid them in a neat bun. She glanced down at the scrubs, smoothed a hand over her top and wished she were dressed a little better. She got her purse and went out to meet Donovan.

He was seated reading a magazine, but tossed it aside and stood when she approached. "Ready?"

Something told her she'd never be ready for a man like him, but she nodded. "Yes."

He placed a hand on the small of her back and guided her toward the exit, the subtle pressure conjuring up memories of how much his touch affected her. And why did he have to look so good?

"So where would you like to go?" Donovan asked, breaking into her thoughts.

"There's a bar and grill not too far from here." She told him the name and street address.

"I know where that is."

"Okay. I'll meet you there." She started in the direction of her car, and he caught her hand.

"Ah, I don't think so." He shook his head. "A gentleman wouldn't let his lady drive to a date, especially a *first* date."

His lady? First date...as in, there would be more? "Oh. I was just thinking it might be easier. Then you wouldn't have to drive back over to drop me off."

He unleashed that captivating smile on her. "Believe me, it's no problem, Simona. Shall we?"

Simona nodded. He continued to hold her hand as they walked across the lot to his car. Donovan stopped next to a late-model black BMW and held the door open. She melted into the butter-soft leather seat as he closed the door.

Donovan got in on the driver's side and started the engine. "It'll be cool in a minute," he said as he turned the air on full blast.

"No problem. Nice car. It still has that new car smell." He must be pretty well-off to afford this type of car. It made her speculate on just what type of job he had.

"Thanks. I've only had it about four months. I figured after eight years it was time for a new one."

She hadn't been on a date in a while and always hated that first date awkwardness. She searched her mind for something to say. "So, you said your arm is okay? Did you see your doctor?"

"Arm's fine. I have an appointment on Thursday. How's your hip?"

"It was sore for a couple of days, but I'm good as new now."

He came to a red light and turned his head in her direction. "Is that right?" His heated gaze roamed lazily over her, lingered at her hip, then moved back up to her face. "That's good to hear," he murmured, focusing his attention back on the road and pulling away.

Simona's pulse spiked. She pulled in a deep breath and stared out the window. His comments were innocent enough, but the accompanying look and sensual undertone warmed her in places she'd forgotten about and reminded her of just what she'd been missing. They lapsed into a companionable silence.

At length Donovan asked, "Is the temperature too cold for you?"

"No. It's fine."

He pressed a button, and a midtempo R & B groove poured from the speakers. The woman singing had an incredible voice, and Simona couldn't resist tapping her fingers to the beat. She was just getting into the song when the car stopped. Donovan helped her out of the car and led her inside the restaurant. Luckily it wasn't too crowded, and they were seated immediately.

After ordering, Donovan leaned back in his chair. "How was your day? I imagine working in the emergency room can be exhausting."

Simona sat, momentarily stunned. She'd just met this man, and he asked about her day. Her ex had never asked about her day—not once in the six months they'd dated. "It's definitely a challenge and exhausting," she answered with a chuckle. "Today wasn't too bad, though."

"How long have you been in nursing?"

"Eight years." She took a sip of her water.

"What made you decide to go into that field?"

"I've always wanted to help people. Growing up, I toyed with becoming a doctor and did some hospital volunteer work in the summers. When I saw how little free time they had—not to mention how long I'd be in school—I changed my mind. I wanted to go into the medical field but still have a life. Nursing is the perfect balance for me."

He leaned forward and rested his arm on the table, as if he was hanging on to her every word. "I think you made the right decision."

"Really? You don't even know me."

"True, but the way you took care of me last Friday says

that you're intelligent and compassionate. And as far as not knowing you…" He reached for her hand and placed a soft kiss on the back. "I plan to change that. I want to know everything there is to know about you, Ms. Simona Andrews."

Simona barely stifled a moan. *This man is too smooth.* Fortunately the server returned with their food because she needed a moment to gather herself. The warmth of his lips against her skin had her fantasizing about how they would feel against other parts of her body.

Donovan stared intently at Simona as she spoke, enjoying the soft melodic sound of her voice, and just being there with her. He reluctantly pulled his gaze away and focused on the food that the server placed in front of him.

During the meal Simona asked, "What about you? What do you do?"

Donovan hesitated briefly. Whenever he disclosed his occupation, most of the women he went out with saw it as an opportunity to score free concert tickets or get closer to the artists. A few had even come right out and asked whether they'd be able to accompany him when he went on tour with Monte and acted offended when he said no. "I'm in music management."

"Music…as in, out in the public? You're a musician?"

He laughed at her reaction. "Hardly. More like sitting in an office with a mound of paperwork this high." He gestured to the top of his head.

"But you work with musicians?"

He studied her. The way she asked the questions gave him pause. Her tone was almost accusatory. "I oversee contracts and a few other things and, yes, I interact with musicians. Does that bother you?"

"No," she answered a little too quickly. "Why music?"

"I love music. My degree is in business economics, and

I had intended to go to law school. But when a buddy of mine asked me to help him out in his business, I saw it as a win-win situation. You must see some crazy stuff in the ER," he said, smoothly changing the subject.

Simona laughed. "Stuff like you wouldn't believe."

While they ate, she regaled him with tales of the emergency room. Donovan couldn't stop laughing at some of the stories she shared, including glued body parts and removal of items from places where objects should never go. When he finally calmed down, he realized it had been a long time since he had actually laughed with a woman. He glanced down at their empty plates and then at his watch. Although he wasn't ready to end the evening, he knew Simona was probably tired. "Would you like anything else? Dessert?"

"No, thank you."

"It's getting late, and I'm sure you need some rest." Donovan paid the bill and escorted Simona back to the car.

On the drive back, she asked, "Who is this singing? Her voice is beautiful."

"Her name is Sheila Martin. She's a relatively new artist."

"I think I'm going to buy some of her music."

This gave him a perfect opening. "Actually, she's performing here a week from Saturday. Would you like to go…that is, if you're not working?"

"Um… I don't know. Wouldn't it be hard to get tickets by now?"

"Tickets aren't a problem. What? You don't like my company?" he teased. "And I've been on my best behavior."

Simona chuckled. "That's not it."

"So, you *do* like my company?"

"A little conceited, aren't you?"

"Nope," he said, slanting her a quick glance. "And you didn't answer the question."

"Yes, I like your company."

"I'm glad. And I'm really enjoying your company, Simona," Donovan added softly. In fact, he enjoyed their time together more than he anticipated, and couldn't wait to do it again.

"Can I check my schedule and let you know about the concert?"

"Absolutely." When they reached the hospital parking lot she directed him to her car, and he helped her out of his and into hers. He dug his phone out of his pocket and extended it to her through her open window. "Can you please put your phone number in?"

She programmed her number and handed it back. "I had a good time tonight, Donovan. Thanks for dinner."

"Anytime. Maybe we can do it again soon."

She smiled and started her car. "I'd like that."

Donovan watched as Simona backed out of the space and cursed under his breath. He'd let her get away twice without kissing her. Making a decision, he jumped into his car and followed her.

One, he wanted to make sure she got home safely, and two, he needed that kiss.

Simona smiled and hummed as she drove, thinking about how much fun she'd had with Donovan tonight. Glancing in her rearview mirror, she let out a startled gasp. Was Donovan following her home? A wave of panic came over her. What was he doing? What if he wanted to come inside? She wasn't ready to tell him about Yasmine.

She spent the entire drive trying to come up with a plan to get him to leave. By the time she pulled up in her driveway, Simona still had no clue what she would tell him.

Taking a deep breath, she shut off the engine and climbed out of the car. Donovan exited his car at the same time.

"I'm not stalking you, if that's what you're thinking," he said, coming toward her with that charming smile.

She couldn't help but laugh. "Well, that's a good thing because—"

He cut her off before she could finish her sentence and her thought. "I just wanted to make sure you got home safely, and…"

"And what?" she asked as he trailed off.

He moved closer and wrapped his arms around her waist. "And I wanted to kiss you good-night."

Simona's pulse spiked. Without waiting for a response, he bent and covered her lips with his. The moment their mouths met, heat flared out in every part of her body. He tangled his tongue with hers unhurriedly, as if he had all night. Her body trembled, and she moaned softly. At length, he lifted his head.

He pressed his lips to hers once more and then whispered, "Good night, Simona." Releasing her, he turned and sauntered back down the driveway.

Simona slumped against her car, heart pounding and legs shaking. She closed her eyes and tried to steady her breathing. When she opened them, he was leaning against his car. "Donovan?"

"I'm just waiting for you to go inside."

Such a gentleman. This man was breaking down her resolve. She walked to her front door and stuck the key into the lock. Before she could open the door, her cell rang. Frowning, she pulled it out and answered it quickly.

"I didn't want you to worry whether I would call or not."

She whirled around to see Donovan standing there with his phone against his ear. "Donovan?"

"Yep. I also realized you need my number so you can let

me know whether you'll attend the concert. Will it work in my favor if I throw in dinner before the show?"

Simona laughed. "Good night, Donovan. I'll let you know."

His deep chuckle rumbled through the line. "Talk to you soon."

She disconnected, waved and went inside. Still smiling, she met Eve coming down the hall holding Yasmine. "Hey, Eve. Hi, Yasmine," she said, reaching for the eager baby. She kissed her niece on the cheek. "Were you waiting for me, little one?"

Simona tried to make sure she kept Yasmine to her scheduled eight-thirty bedtime. It was only twenty minutes past that time, and she figured her niece was waiting for their usual bedtime ritual of reading, singing, back rub and kissing the two small stuffed animals that slept in the corner of the crib.

"Let me put her to bed, and I'll be right back," she said to Eve.

"Take your time. I'll be waiting to hear all about that dinner date."

Simona shook her head and continued down the hall to Yasmine's bedroom. She placed her purse on the dresser and sat in the rocking chair. Yasmine immediately lifted her arms. "Okay. I know you want to sing 'Itsy Bitsy Spider.'" She sang a jazzed-up version of the tune, plus "Jesus Loves Me" before rising to place the baby in her crib.

They played the kissing game. Yasmine giggled and babbled, "Mamamama," warming Simona's heart. The little girl was asleep within minutes of the back rub.

Simona made sure the monitor was turned on and left silently. Eve was sitting at the dining room table with a book open, scribbling furiously. She sat across from her. "How're classes going?"

Eve put the pen down and removed her glasses. "Girl,

somebody should have warned me that brain cells die after thirty. I was always a good student, but this thirty-four-year-old brain ain't what it used to be. This master's program in psychology is no joke. If I ever get the notion to go back for a doctorate, please smack me upside the head." They both laughed. "Enough of that." She leaned forward with her head propped in her elbows. "I want to hear about your dinner with Donovan."

"There's not much to tell. We just went to a bar and grill."

"What kind of car does he drive, and what does he do?"

"He drives a BMW and works in music management. He says he works in the office, but knows some musicians."

"Really?"

"Yeah. He's a really nice guy, but I don't want a repeat of what happened before."

"You can't compare Donovan to Travis."

Simona cringed at the mention of her ex. She had met the up-and-coming actor at a local theater in San Francisco where a friend was also performing. Her friend had invited Simona to hang out with the cast after the show. Travis Jacobs had been pleasant and likeable, and before she knew it, they were a couple. Initially, things had been great. But as the months rolled by it became less about *them* and more about *him*, and his true egotistical nature was on display for the world to see. Every date became a photo op, and after six months she called it quits.

Rather than let it go, Travis spun it to insinuate that he'd initiated their breakup and used it as an opportunity to further his career, making it sound as if he was devastated by the breakup—he had the nerve to shed a tear during an interview—and accused her of being jealous of his fame.

After several months of dodging the cameras, she'd quit the job she loved and relocated to LA. It didn't help that Simona was dealing with her sister's death and concerned about her niece.

"Simona?" Eve gently prodded.

"I know. But I can't do that again. Travis made my life a living hell. I couldn't go anywhere without a camera in my face. And now I have Yasmine."

"Did you tell Donovan about her?"

"No. We barely know each other, and I don't want to start bringing all kinds of men around. Besides, most men don't want to be saddled with a woman who has a child."

"I can see your point about not wanting to bring lots of men around her, but what if Donovan wants to continue seeing you? How long are you going to hide her from him?"

"I don't know what I'll do. He asked me to go to a concert next weekend."

Eve stood. "Well, if you decide to go to the concert, I'll be happy to babysit. But don't wait too long to tell him." She gathered up her book and papers and put them into a tote. "Oh, your grandmother called."

"Okay. Thanks. I'll call her tomorrow."

She saw Eve to the door, then came back and collapsed on the sofa. "And this is why I don't date," she muttered, rubbing her temples.

Leaning back, Simona replayed every detail of the evening in her head. She laughed, remembering Donovan's phone call outside. Her smile faded and she groaned. He hadn't said a lot about his job, just that he worked in an office. But what did he really do?

As much as she had enjoyed her time with Donovan tonight, she needed to put the brakes on whatever was going on between them. She wasn't ready to put herself out there again, especially with someone who possibly lived in the public eye.

Chapter 5

Donovan's thumb hovered over the telephone number on his screen for several seconds before he pressed the home button and tossed the phone on his desk. It had been three days since he had seen or spoken to Simona and exactly one week since they met. He hadn't been able to stop thinking about her or the kiss. He'd known instinctively he would enjoy kissing her but never expected the onslaught of emotions that accompanied the act. They were the same feelings he'd had at the hospital last week. And, for the first time in over two years, he felt the stirrings of something more than a passing fling. She made him laugh and he chuckled, recalling some of the stories she'd told him.

Simona still hadn't called to let him know if she would accompany him to Sheila's concert. He was anxious to call her, but didn't want to come on too strong. From the questions she asked about his job, he sensed some hesitancy on her part and wondered why. Donovan glanced over at the wall clock—four thirty. He still had work to do, and he wanted to leave at a reasonable time so he could stop by Terrence and Janae's to see his little goddaughter. He reined in his thoughts and refocused on the papers in front of him. By the time he looked up again, over an hour had passed. He stood, stretched and went to the outer office where his secretary sat clicking away on the computer.

"You about ready to wrap it up, Monique?"

She paused. "Yes. I just want to print this last contract for Brad. He said he'd be by to pick it up in a few minutes."

On the heels of her statement, Brad, who headed up the label's legal department, entered with his wife, Audrey, director of Human Resources. Both were friends from college.

"Your ears must have been burning," Donovan said.

"What? You're talking about me again?" Brad asked with a laugh. He turned to his wife. "See, babe, I told you I'm the man."

Audrey rolled her eyes. "Whatever. Just get what you came for so we can go. You have two hours to finish that stuff. We are *not* taking any work this weekend."

Donovan laughed. "Finally getting that trip to San Francisco in, huh? Brad, make sure you take her on the sunset cruise," he added with a wink.

"We're doing that and more," she said with a sly smile.

Brad leaned down and gave her a quick kiss.

Donovan held up his hands. "TMI, T-M-I! Monique, hurry up and give Brad those papers before they burn my office down." He was glad to see that they were still so much in love after being together for more than a decade. He felt a pang of jealousy.

"Are you going to be here much longer, Donovan?" Brad asked as he collected the papers from Monique.

"No. I'm going to see my beautiful goddaughter."

"We went by for a few minutes last night," Audrey said

excitedly. "And you're right, she's a cutie. But we'd better get going."

"Have fun."

"We will." Brad and Audrey said their goodbyes, with Monique close behind.

Donovan left a few minutes later, and it took him almost an hour to get to Terrence's with rush-hour traffic.

"What's up, D? Come on in," Terrence said, bringing Donovan in for their customary hug.

"Hey." He followed Terrence to the family room and stretched out on the sofa.

"You look exhausted. Is everything going okay?"

"Yeah, fine. I was thinking we might need to hire someone else to help out, especially since I figure you'll be spending less time at the office. And you'll be touring again soon."

Terrence sighed. "I've been thinking about that, too. But I don't want to bring in someone at the executive level who starts trying to tell me my business."

"I know. I have an idea I want to run by you." He sat up. "Monique has been doing a great job fielding calls, making sure things run smoothly with the clients and generally helping me out with the departments. She just graduated in May with her degree in business, and I think she'd make a helluva manager."

"I like it, but what about the secretarial stuff? That leaves only one person to handle that."

"We can either move someone from another department or hire from outside. I can talk to Audrey about it next week if you're cool with it."

Terrence sat quietly, mulling over the proposition, then slowly nodded. "Okay."

"Good. Now that we're done with work, where's Janae and Nadia?"

"Janae was feeding her when I came down. Let me see if she's done." He got to his feet and went upstairs.

While he was gone, Donovan leaned back and closed his eyes. Thoughts of Simona drifted through his mind. It was after seven, so he assumed she was off work, unless she was working overtime as she had last Friday. How did she spend her weekends? What kinds of things did she like to do? He thought about how her beautiful smile and soft laughter made his heart beat a little faster. It had been a long while since a woman affected him in this way, and it surprised him just how much he wanted to see her again.

Donovan blew out a long breath. Maybe it was time for him to let his guard down some. For two long years he had resisted allowing a woman into his heart—he didn't want to feel the pain of betrayal again. Back when Terrence was fighting his attraction to Janae, Donovan had accused his friend of punishing all women for the actions of one. But he was no better. He talked a good game, but this time his heart was on the line.

"Hi, Donovan."

He opened his eyes and stood at the sound of Janae's voice. "Hey, Janae. How're you feeling?" he asked, kissing her cheek.

"Tired, of course," she said with a laugh, "but I'm enjoying it. You look exhausted."

"It's been a hectic couple of weeks."

"I can imagine. Well, I know you're anxious to hold Nadia. I'm going to head back upstairs. I know you and Terrence have a lot to catch up on." She carefully transferred the baby.

"I'll walk you up, sweetheart," Terrence said, placing his arm around her shoulders. "Will you be okay alone for a minute, Donovan?"

Donovan shot him a look. "Of course. Nadia and I need time to get acquainted, so don't hurry back."

Janae laughed as she and Terrence left the room.

Donovan cradled Nadia close to his heart and placed a gentle kiss on her forehead. Just like the first time he held her, a rush of emotions flooded him, along with a flashback of what should have been. Had his little one survived, he or she would be a year and a half now. He pushed down the painful memories and stared at the baby who had her eyes fixed on him.

"Hey, Nadia. I think you've gotten more beautiful since the last time I saw you. How are you liking this world so far?" She stretched and yawned. "That well, huh?" he said with a chuckle. "I know you've got great parents, but if you ever need anything, you can call me and Uncle Donovan will be right there, okay?" He sang quietly and rocked her slowly. After a moment, she closed her eyes. Donovan kept up the rocking motion while singing.

"I see you still got it," Terrence said, coming up behind him. "I could use another session singer for the new project I'm working on."

Donovan turned and snorted. "I don't think so. I only did those background lyrics for the first two CDs because you were just starting out, and we were trying to save money. But since you're all rich and famous now, you can hire somebody. I like my job just fine." He cocked his head to the side. "You know, I don't think I was ever paid for my services."

Terrence laughed softly. "Whatever. Boy, you've been paid that and more." He gestured to Donovan's arm. "What happened?"

Donovan glanced down at his arm. He had an appointment to remove the stitches on Monday, and he couldn't wait. The itching was driving him crazy. The burn was healing nicely and barely noticeable. "I got it caught on a coffee cart at the hospital while trying to keep it from falling last Friday night after I left you." He gave Terrence the details about what happened.

"I'm guessing you went to the emergency room. That had to be a fun wait, especially on a Friday night."

"Yeah, but I didn't have to wait."

Terrence lifted a brow. "How did you manage that?"

"I bypassed all the waiting because of the nurse I kept from falling. She was really sweet."

"Really? Did you get her name?"

"Yes, and we went out to dinner on Tuesday."

Terrence smiled. "I see. It's about time."

"Shut up," Donovan said, but he was smiling.

"Oh, hell naw. You were all up in my business when I was dating Janae. It's payback, my brother. You've hardly dated since Rolanda."

Donovan's smile faded, and he reclaimed his seat on the couch, adjusting the baby in his arms.

Terrence sat in a chair across from him. "What's going on, Donovan? We've been friends for a long time, and I know something is up. What happened with Rolanda?"

Donovan's jaw tightened. He did not want to relive that time, and felt the anger rising. "I trusted her, and she broke that trust." Nadia fussed a little and squirmed in his arms.

Terrence rose. "Let me go put her down, then we're going to talk."

Donovan kissed Nadia once more and passed her off to her father. He'd done a good job keeping the pain of his heartbreak at bay, but Nadia's birth and meeting Simona seemed to bring everything to the surface. Terrence's voice drew him out of his reverie.

"All right. Let's hear it, D," Terrence said, dropping down into the chair he had vacated minutes earlier.

Donovan leaned forward and braced his forearms on his knees. "Remember when we got back from San Francisco the weekend you met Janae?"

Terrence frowned, then nodded. "When you took a few days off? I recall you leaving in the middle of the day after receiving a phone call—one you never mentioned again."

"Yeah. The call was from a nurse at UCLA Medical Center. She wanted to make sure Rolanda was doing well after her *procedure*."

Terrence's brow rose. "What kind of procedure?" he asked hesitantly.

"She'd had a miscarriage at eleven weeks."

"Wow. I had no idea she was pregnant."

"Neither did I," Donovan replied solemnly. "I would've never known had the nurse not called me by mistake. I guess Rolanda put my name down as an emergency contact when she went in."

"What did she say when you confronted her?"

"Basically that it was none of my business. Rolanda wasn't too upset about it because she didn't really want to have kids. I asked her what she would have done if she hadn't miscarried—if she would have told me."

"And she said?"

"She said she didn't know."

"How in the hell did she think she'd be able to keep that from you? At some point, there'd be no way you *couldn't* know."

Donovan jumped up from the couch, ran his hand over his head and paced the floor. "I know that, T, and that's what pissed me off the most. For all I know, she might have…" He trailed off, not wanting to finish the thought.

"I'm sorry. I don't know what to say."

"You know what's really crazy? Before that, I'd never thought too much about having children or being a father. But since then I haven't stopped thinking about it. And after holding Nadia and seeing the way you are with her, I want the same thing. The only problem is, I don't know if I can let myself get close enough to another woman."

"What about the nurse you went out with? What's her name?"

"Simona Andrews. I like her. She's caring, compassionate and fun to be with, but—"

Terrence stood. "Well, like you told me, you can't punish all women for the actions of one. She might be the woman you need."

Donovan folded his arms. "Had I known you'd be throwing this crap back in my face, I'd have kept my mouth shut," he muttered.

Terrence laughed. "Hey, for the record, you were right. It was great advice. I never thought I would fall in love, didn't want to. But I can't tell you how much Janae has changed my life for the better." He shook his head and placed his hand over his heart. "I love my girls."

"I know, and I'm happy for you."

"So, do you plan to see Simona again?"

"I invited her to Sheila's concert next Saturday, but she hasn't said whether she'll go or not."

"Be sure to invite her to the barbecue. It's two weeks after the concert."

"We'll see. She seemed a little weird or—I can't put my finger on it—when I told her what I do."

Terrence shrugged. "It's better than her asking you for concert tickets, autographs and entry to release parties before you can get her name."

Donovan smiled. "True dat. On that note, I'm outta here." He walked to the front door, with Terrence following. "I'll talk to you next week."

"I hope things work out with you and Simona. Let me know if you decide to bring her to the party."

"Will do." Donovan turned and loped down the steps to his car. He had driven only a short distance when his cell rang. He engaged the Bluetooth. "Hello."

"Donovan. Hi, it's Simona. Did I catch you at a bad time?"

"Not at all. How are you?"

"I'm good. I was calling to let you know I'll be available to go to the concert."

He smiled. "Glad to hear it. Was it the dinner offer that put me over the top?"

Her throaty laughter came through the line. "No. And you don't have to take me to dinner. The concert will be enough."

"And if I want to take you to dinner, too?"

"I have some things to take care of earlier. What time does the concert start?"

"Eight. If you're busy, we can save the dinner for another time."

"That would be better, thanks. So...um...I'll let you get back to doing whatever you were doing."

"Driving."

"What?"

"I'm driving."

"Oh. Well, drive safely."

"Always."

"I'll talk to you later. Good night."

"Night." Donovan disconnected and drummed his fingers on the steering wheel. He was still wary of opening himself up to another woman. But he didn't plan to let that stop him from going after the woman he wanted. And he wanted Simona.

Chapter 6

Simona replaced the cordless phone on the table and released a deep sigh. Each time she talked to Donovan chipped away more at her resolve. She was drawn to this man despite her best efforts to stay away. There was no way she should have agreed to attend the concert with him, especially since she was trying to keep her life simple. But his sexy voice, laughter and considerate manner made it difficult to say no. He had even left her a message yesterday wishing her a good day. Then there was that kiss... whoa! The way he'd kissed her had every molecule in her body ready to wave the white flag and surrender.

The sound of giggling drew her out of her lustful thoughts. She glanced over to where Yasmine sat on the floor playing.

Simona slid off the couch and onto the floor next to her. "What are you giggling about?" Yasmine was such a happy baby. She rarely cried unless something was wrong. Simona considered herself lucky.

"Mamamama." Yasmine turned, braced her arms on Simona's thigh and pulled to standing. Giving Simona a wide grin, showing her eight teeth, she clapped her hands.

Simona clapped along and said, "Yay! You're such a big girl." Yasmine had been walking for only a few weeks, but was getting faster every day, and childproofing had taken on new meaning. Simona scooped her up just as the little girl made it across the room to the table and reached for the phone. "Oh, no you don't," Simona said with a laugh. "I'm not paying for any calls made to Africa or China."

Yasmine's squeals of delight filled Simona's heart. She just wished her sister were here to share it.

Their laughter was interrupted when the phone rang. Simona paused, thinking Donovan was calling back. She picked up the phone, checked the display and smiled upon seeing her grandmother's number.

"Hey, Nana."

"Hi, Simona. Sorry I missed your call the other night. Prayer meeting and Bible study ran over."

"It's no problem."

"I planned to call you back last night, but Deacon Mitchell asked me to dinner."

"Oooh, go, Nana! You've got a boyfriend?" At seventy years old, Frances Walker still possessed the ability to turn the heads of men at least a decade younger. She exercised, danced and lived a full life.

Her grandmother giggled. "Hush, girl. No. We just went out for a nice dinner."

"Uh-huh, tell me anything. I might have to make a trip up there to check him out."

"He's a nice man. Been widowed about ten years. We had a nice time. I'm not the only one going out on dates, from what I heard," she added with a chuckle. "You need to find a nice young man."

"You always say that."

"And I'm always right. What's his name, and where did you meet him?"

"His name is Donovan, and I met him at the hospital." She told her grandmother what happened with the cart.

"Is he a cutie-pie?"

Simona shook her head. "Yes, Nana, he's a cutie-pie."

"Does he have a good job?"

"I guess so. He works in music management—in an office—but I'm still a little unsure about exactly what it is he does. And after Travis, I want to steer clear of anyone who might be popular."

"Oh, sweetheart. You can't base every man on how Travis behaved. I never liked him. Always putting on airs."

Her grandmother had always said there was something about Travis that didn't ring true, and Simona wished she had listened.

"From what Eve told me, it doesn't sound like this young man is the same."

Eve talks too much. "No, he isn't."

"Well, it won't hurt to spend some time with him."

"Maybe."

"You have a good head on your shoulders, so it'll be all right. How's my great-granddaughter? I saw the beautiful pictures. She looks just like her mama at that age."

"She's growing so fast. And yes, she does."

"Have you talked to your mother?"

"Not since she called to tell me she was going to Cancun with Roy, or Rob, or whoever it is this time."

Frances sighed heavily. "I wish she would just settle down with one man. She's getting too old for this nonsense."

Simona chuckled. Since her parents' divorce fifteen years ago, her mother changed men almost as often as she changed her clothes. "Hopefully he's the one. She did say she was in love this time." Simona leaned over and plucked a penny out of Yasmine's hand before she could get it to her mouth and was rewarded with a loud wail.

"Hmph. That's a first. What did you do to my baby?"

"Kept her from eating a penny. I don't know how she finds these things. I try to make sure I don't miss anything, but she finds the tiniest specks."

"All babies are like that. Go take care of her. We'll talk soon. Love you, baby."

"Love you, too, Nana." She hung up, tossed the phone on the couch and picked up Yasmine. "Okay, little miss, it's bath and bedtime for you."

After putting Yasmine to bed, Simona showered and got into bed. She picked up the mystery novel she'd been trying to finish for the past two weeks. Two pages in, her mind went back to its favorite subject of late—Donovan. With his killer smile, sexy dimple and mesmerizing eyes, it was going to take every ounce of willpower she had to resist him. Her eyes slid closed as she recalled his hard body pressed against hers, the way his hand caressed her back, the intensity of his kiss. Even now, the thought of his soft, warm lips against hers sent a wave of desire through her. And, once again, thoughts of those same lips moving over her body seeped into her fantasy.

Simona's eyes snapped open and she groaned. The man had kissed her only once and had her all hot and bothered. It was just a simple good-night kiss. Nothing more.

Yeah, but it was the best kiss of your life, good-night or otherwise, her mind argued.

She ignored the errant thought. Best kiss or not, she needed to maintain her distance, and she had only a short time to figure out how to get it done.

Simona rushed around her bedroom trying to get dressed. Instead of picking her up at seven fifteen as planned, Donovan had called and asked if she could be ready an hour earlier because he had to stop at his office first. Her bed looked as if it had been hit by a tornado, with the many outfits she had tried on and discarded. She threw up her hands. "Why is this so hard? It's just a date."

Yasmine raised her arms and giggled.

"Oh, so you think this is funny, huh?" The doorbell rang. "Let's go get the door." She opened the door to Eve. "Hey."

"You're not dressed yet?" Eve asked as she entered and took Yasmine. "Donovan is going to be here in half an hour."

"I know. I can't decide what to wear," Simona said, going back to her room with Eve following. When they got to the room, Eve laughed.

"Girl, you have more clothes on the bed than in your closet. It's a concert. You'll be fine wearing a dress or pants. What is Donovan wearing?"

"I have no idea. I didn't ask." She held up a cap-sleeve, curve-hugging royal blue dress, turning it one way, then another.

"That's nice. Put it on. Yasmine and I will be waiting." Eve walked out, closing the door behind her.

Simona slipped into the dress, applied light makeup and sat on the edge of the bed to put on her shoes. The strappy black sandals added four inches to her five-foot-six-inch frame. She stood in front of her floor-length mirror and surveyed the look. Her stomach wasn't as flat as she liked, but the ruched design of the dress concealed it perfectly. She added large silver hoop earrings and released the clip on her braids. Tonight she decided to leave her hair down. It had been a while since she'd gone on a date, and she looked forward to a nice evening out. Smiling, she picked up her small black shoulder bag and left the room.

"You look great, Simona," Eve said when Simona entered the living room.

"Thanks." She glanced down at her watch. Donovan would be arriving any minute.

"If Donovan is the gentleman I think he is, he'll be ringing that doorbell shortly."

Simona nodded. "I still haven't decided whether this is leading anywhere, so I'd rather not tell him about Yasmine yet."

"We'll wait in the bedroom until you leave, but you need to hurry up and decide."

"I know, and I will. Thanks, Eve." The doorbell rang, and Simona's belly fluttered. She waited until Eve had taken Yasmine into the bedroom before going to the door.

When she opened it, the sight of Donovan standing there in all his handsomeness with a single long-stemmed yellow rose made her heart skip a beat.

"Wow! You look absolutely beautiful," he said, extending the rose.

"Thank you, and thank you for the rose. It's lovely. You don't look so bad yourself." Instead of the dress shirt he had worn the past two times she'd seen him, tonight he had on a pale gray silk T-shirt that displayed his muscular biceps paired with navy trousers. "I'm ready. I know you have to make a stop first." She stepped out onto the porch and closed the door behind her.

He gave her a curious look and guided her to his car. Starting the engine, he glanced her way, letting his eyes linger on her bare legs before raising them to meet her eyes. "I hope the change in time didn't interfere with your plans."

"No, you're fine. Do you have to pick up some work?"

"Nope. I left the tickets sitting on my desk."

Simona chuckled. "Well, yeah, I guess we'll need those."

Donovan shook his head. "I can't believe I did that."

"It happens to the best of us." She settled in for the

ride, and they made small talk until he arrived at an office building.

He parked in the garage, hopped out and came around to her side. "It should only take a minute."

For a brief moment she considered waiting in the car, but curiosity got the best of her. She wanted to see exactly where he worked. Inside the elevator he pressed the button for the sixth floor. The car rose swiftly, and when the doors opened, Donovan guided her across highly polished floors to a hallway. An empty reception desk sat at the entrance, with RC Productions written in large gold letters on the wall behind it.

They stopped at an office near the far end of the hall. Her gaze narrowed upon reading the nameplate: Donovan Wright, Executive Vice President. So much for him just overseeing a few departments.

He unlocked the door and flipped a switch, illuminating a large outer office, which she assumed belonged to his secretary. The inner office was even larger and had a small conference table with seating for six over to one side. A huge mahogany desk sat on the opposite side. She wandered around the room, looking at the gold and platinum records hanging on the wall, and felt a measure of unease.

"I thought you said you weren't a recording artist."

"I'm not. Most of the offices have them." He held up the tickets.

Simona pointed to one then another. "So, the D. E. Wright inscribed on this one and this one is not you?"

He sighed. "Yes, it is, but only because I was one of the writers on the song." Coming to where she stood, Donovan gathered her in his arms. "What's going on, Simona? Every time the topic of my job comes up, you seem… I don't know."

Not ready to share her past with him, she said, "I'm just curious, that's all."

"I can assure you I am not a singer. The only reason my name is on it is because the artist insisted."

She wanted to believe him, and he hadn't given her any reason to think he was someone other than who he said. But the thought of having a repeat of her last relationship made her think that this might be their last date.

He tilted her chin. "Simona, are you sure there's nothing bothering you? I really like you, and I'm hoping we can spend more time together."

Staring into his earnest eyes, she heard herself say, "So do I." *So much for that little self-speech about this being the last date.* He lowered his head and placed a soft kiss on her lips. She leaned up and impulsively ran her tongue across his bottom lip. He captured it with lightning speed. She heard him groan as he deepened the kiss. His hands roamed down her back and over her hips. Simona felt his fingers slip beneath the hem of her dress to caress her bare thigh, and she moaned softly.

He transferred his kisses to her jaw, the curve of her neck and shoulder. "I can't get over how amazing you look in this dress," Donovan murmured, moving back to her mouth.

Simona's body trembled with a need unlike anything she had ever experienced. She clung to him as his mouth plundered hers and his hand moved higher up her thigh, sending shockwaves of pleasure through her.

"Donovan," she whispered, breaking off the kiss. Her chest heaved as she tried to slow her breathing. His eyes glittered with desire, and she closed hers so he wouldn't see the longing in them.

"We'd better get out of here," Donovan said, his breathing as labored as hers. He locked the office and led her back to the garage.

Simona sat in the car with her hands clasped together in her lap, still attempting to bring her rampant emotions under control—not to mention the insistent throbbing between her thighs, the pounding of her heart in her chest. Neither spoke much during the drive, giving her some time to think. She needed to get herself together. She couldn't afford to fall so easily for this man, no matter how fine he was or how his kisses made her feel.

Her attention was drawn to all the traffic leading to Club Nokia. Even though she had lived in LA for a year, Simona hadn't explored her new city. She spotted Staples Center, JW Marriott and a movie theater, among other things.

"I never knew all this was here," she said.

"You've never been over here?"

"No, I've only lived in LA for a year."

Donovan slanted her a quick glance. "Really? I thought you grew up here. Where are you from?"

"Oakland."

"What made you move here?"

"I needed a change, and taking the job here was a great learning opportunity, so the decision was easy." It wasn't a total lie.

He nodded. "Have you visited many places since you've been here?"

"Actually, this is the first place I've gone, aside from a few local restaurants."

"Not even Disneyland?" he asked with a smile.

She returned his smile. "Not even Disneyland. The only amusement park I've been to is Six Flags in Vallejo."

"Aw, Simona, you have to go to Disneyland at least once." He parked in the underground lot of the club and rotated his body toward her. "I tell you what, since you're a relative newcomer to LA, how about I show you around? We can go to Disneyland and any other place you want to visit. What do you say?"

He really needed to stop smiling at her. That darn dim-

ple and those sparkling eyes in his too-fine face melted
any resistance she had built up on the ride here. "Okay."

"Great. We'll coordinate our schedules."

When he got out of the car, Simona banged her head
softly against the seat and groaned. *How hard is it to say
the word* no, *Simona?* her inner self chastised. *Or to at
least say you'll think about it.* He made it so easy to say
yes. At the rate she was going, she would be totally under
his spell before the night ended, or worse…falling in love.

Chapter 7

Donovan held Simona's hand as they entered the theater. He was surprised to learn Simona had not grown up in LA, but it would be his supreme pleasure to escort her around town. This gave him the chance to spend time with her, getting to know her under the guise of being a good host.

Glancing at her, he couldn't get over how gorgeous she looked in that body-hugging dress. He had almost swallowed his tongue when she opened the door. Holding her the first night they had kissed, he'd felt her curves. However, he had no idea those loose-fitting scrubs hid a body that sexy. Remembering the feel of her silky bare thigh beneath his fingers and the seductive taste of her kiss sent a jolt directly to his groin, and Donovan tried to force his thoughts elsewhere as he guided her down the aisle. They were seated with ten minutes to spare.

"How did you get front row seats?" Simona asked, cutting into his musings. "Is this another perk of your job?"

He hesitated briefly before nodding. Donovan still

sensed that she had been less than forthcoming about her thoughts regarding his job. She wasn't telling him something, and he wondered why she was so uncomfortable. "Sheila Martin is one of the label's artists. She's been with us close to two years, and this is her first project. She's had great reviews and sold out in smaller venues, so her manager wanted to try something larger. From what I understand, this will be a sellout, as well."

Simona nodded. "She has an amazing voice. Reminds me of Jill Scott or Gladys Knight—not so much in style, but in the strength of her voice."

"In other words, like an old-school R & B singer."

"Exactly," Simona answered with a smile.

The lights went down, and Sheila hit the stage. Throughout the concert, Donovan stole glances at Simona. She seemed to be enjoying herself, if the way she moved her body in time with the beat was any indication. The last woman he had taken to a concert bugged him the entire time about whether he had backstage passes, and if there were any after-parties. By the time the concert had ended, he was so irritated that he'd taken her home as soon as the last song was over and dropped her off with a "don't call me, I'll call you" line and immediately blocked her number from his cell. Since that date a year ago, he had been leery of disclosing his true job and had gone out with only a few women, none of whom held his attention like the one sitting next to him.

Donovan could list a dozen reasons he should tread lightly where Simona was concerned—the possibility of having his heart broken topped the list—but for the first time in his life he felt like a car careening out of control with no brakes. He turned his attention back to the music.

"Wow, she was great," Simona said when the concert ended. "I'm even more anxious to add her to my collection."

"Actually, you can purchase one tonight, if you want. They'll be selling autographed copies in one of the VIP rooms shortly. And before you ask, yes, I'll have access before they let the general public in. Consider it another perk. Would you like to go?"

"Are there going to be lots of media and cameras?"

"Probably."

"Then no."

Donovan angled his head thoughtfully. Her curt reply gave him pause. "Are you camera shy?"

"Something like that," Simona mumbled. "I can just buy it when I go shopping, or download it."

A cryptic response. "I promise not to let anyone come near you with a camera. We can still get it now, if you want. We'll be in and out before they start." He grasped her hand and started in the direction of the VIP room.

"Donovan, you don't have to do that. It's fine. Really."

He slowed his steps. "Is there something more I need to know other than you just being camera shy?"

"I just like my privacy. Besides, I don't want crazy photos or anything to negatively impact my job," she added with a nervous chuckle.

He stared at her for a long moment, not believing one word. She wasn't telling him something…the slight trembling in her hand said so. Donovan brought her hand to his lips and placed a soft kiss on the back. He wanted to know what had happened, but dropped the subject for now. They were still getting to know each other, and hopefully she would confide in him one day. But for now, he wanted her to trust him. "Like I said, we can be in and out quickly, but if you're uncomfortable, we can skip it."

She smiled up at him. "I'm fine. Let's go."

Donovan searched her face for the truth and finally nodded. When they reached the VIP room, two security guards were at the door, one he recognized from previous visits.

"Well, well, if it isn't Donovan Wright. How you doing, man? Long time, no see."

"How's it going, Percy?" he said, reaching out to shake the man's hand. "Dale and Sheila in there yet?"

"Just made it." He unlocked the door and waved them in. "You and your lady staying for the party?"

"No. I just want to congratulate Sheila. What time are you letting the media in?"

Percy checked his watch. "About fifteen minutes," he said, and closed the door behind Donovan and Simona.

Donovan grasped Simona's hand and guided her to the opposite side of the room where a few people stood setting up the CDs. "I want to introduce you to Sheila and her manager, Dale. Then we'll get your CD and be out in five minutes. How does that sound?"

"It sounds good." She stopped walking and squeezed his hand. "Thank you for understanding, Donovan."

Her soft smile and relieved expression tugged on his heart, and he tried to push down the sensation. He made the introductions and Simona purchased a CD, which Sheila gladly signed. As they were leaving, Sheila's manager asked to speak with him briefly.

"This won't take long, Simona," he told her. Donovan took in Simona's nervous expression and mentally sighed. On the one hand, he'd promised Simona they'd be done quickly. On the other, this was part of his job, and he prided himself on ensuring he was accessible to all RC Productions clients.

Simona stood anxiously off to the side and took a quick peek at her watch, hoping Donovan would finish his conversation soon, though she couldn't be mad at him for doing his job. It wasn't his fault the thought of someone from the media taking her picture and linking her back to her ex freaked her out. No, that honor belonged to Travis, she thought sarcastically.

Loud voices coming from the other side of the room startled her. A stream of people entered the room. Her panicked gaze sought out Donovan, but he was quickly swallowed up by the influx of fans eager to meet Sheila Martin. Her heart raced, and she moved to a corner. Moments later, a strong arm circled her waist.

"Come on, baby. Let's go," Donovan whispered close to her ear.

They threaded their way through the crowd, and she breathed a sigh of relief once they exited the club.

He slung an arm around her shoulder. "Are you okay?"

"I'm fine—it was just all those people at the end had me feeling a little claustrophobic," she answered brightly, praying Donovan wouldn't know how rattled she had gotten. Simona had no desire to rehash the details of her past. "It's nice that Sheila's made such an impact with her music, this being her first CD."

"She's pretty happy about it, too. Can I tempt you into getting some dessert?"

Simona laughed. "Tempting, but I'd better not."

"How about some coffee or tea? There's a Starbucks up the street."

"Okay. Starbucks will work." It was already after ten, and she didn't want to be out much longer. Forty-five minutes later, Donovan, seemingly reluctant, escorted her to the car.

"I'm really not ready to end the evening, but I'd better get you home," he said with a heavy sigh.

Truth be told, Simona didn't want the evening to end, either. It had been a long time since she had enjoyed being with a man, but she needed to get home to her niece. She still hadn't decided how to tell Donovan about Yasmine. Tonight had made her more certain that a relationship between them could never happen. As much as she enjoyed being with him, she didn't want to risk another chance at her quiet life being disrupted.

On the drive, Simona tried to come up with a good reason to give Donovan as to why she couldn't see him again, but drew a blank. She had never had a problem telling a man she didn't want to see him in the past. Then again, she'd never met a man like Donovan—a man whose very presence commanded a room and who was both strong and gentle at the same time. Why couldn't he have a nice, quiet job? His hand settled on top of hers.

"Simona?"

"I'm sorry. Did you say something?"

"I was just asking if you were okay. You seemed to be in another world over there."

She wished they were in another world. "I'm fine. Just thinking about how much fun I had tonight."

"I'm glad." He pulled into her driveway, cut the engine and rotated in his seat to face her. "A buddy of mine is having a barbecue a week from Saturday, and I'd like to invite you. It'll be very low key."

"Donovan, I…" She trailed off at the hopeful expression on his face.

"Please. His grandmother is on a mission to fix me up with the granddaughter of one of her friends. Can you help a brother out?" He gave her a sad expression.

She turned her head to hide her smile. *Why can't I tell this man no?* Turning back, she asked, "All right. What time?"

Donovan unleashed his full dimpled smile. "Great! Thank you. Everything's going to start around one. I'll pick you up around twelve forty-five." He hopped out of the car and came to her side of the car. Pulling Simona to her feet, he brushed a kiss across her lips. "I really appreciate you helping me out. Although, I have to confess, I just want to spend more time with you." He took her hand and led her up the walkway.

Simona wanted to spend more time with him, too, but she couldn't tell him that. What she *should* say is that the barbecue would be their last date. Somehow, she couldn't get her mouth to form those words, either. When they got to her front door, she looked up at him. "Thank you for a nice evening, Donovan."

"I enjoyed being with you," Donovan said, bending to kiss her.

The moment their mouths met, he slid his tongue between her parted lips and latched on to hers. Pulling her closer, he angled his head and deepened the kiss, sending shockwaves of pleasure through her body. Simona moaned and gripped his shoulders when she felt the solid bulge of his erection against her belly. She knew she should stop him, but every coherent thought went right out the window. Her body trembled, and she felt his body shudder.

Breaking off the kiss, he rested his forehead against hers. "I'm trying to take this slow, but I want to make love to you, Simona, and if we stand here one minute longer..." He clenched his jaw, seemingly trying to gain control.

Taking her keys, he unlocked and opened the door. Good thing, because her body was so on fire that her hands were shaking.

"Good night. I'll call you." He placed a quick kiss on her lips, turned and hurried down the walk.

She shut the door behind her and slumped against it. How in the world was she ever going to walk away from Donovan? Closing her eyes, she willed her body calm.

"Is everything okay, Simona?"

She jumped, and her eyes snapped open when she heard Eve's voice from the living room couch. She nodded.

A knowing grin curved Eve's mouth. She folded her arms. "So, Donovan must be a great kisser."

Simona felt a rush of heat to her face.

"You don't have to answer. I peeked out the curtains when he picked you up earlier. A man that fine probably has the market cornered on how to please a woman."

She pushed off the door. "Yeah. Something like that," she mumbled.

"I thought for sure you'd invite him in," Eve said.

"I...I can't."

"Don't tell me you still haven't told him about Yasmine."

Simona shook her head guiltily.

Eve threw up her hands. "Come on, Simona. From what I see, the two of you are getting closer, and you can't keep something like this from him."

"I know, I know. But I can't let him get too close. He's more in the public eye than I thought." She told Eve about going to his office at the recording label and the VIP party. "When Donovan told me about his job initially, he made it sound like he was just some kind of office manager, but he's the *executive vice president*! I had planned for tonight to be our last date, but somehow I agreed to go to a barbecue with him in two weeks." Simona groaned.

Eve chuckled. "It was those kisses."

Despite her frustration, Simona laughed. "Yeah, that, those seductive light brown eyes and that damn dimple in his left cheek."

"Ooh. Does he have an older brother?" They looked at each other and collapsed in a fit of laughter. When they calmed down, Eve stood. "Let me go home." At the door, she hugged Simona. "Honey, you need to talk to Donovan. From what you told me, it doesn't sound like he's cocky about his popularity."

"No, he isn't." Thinking back, if anything, he seemed to downplay it.

"Then maybe you should think twice about breaking things off. Good men are hard to find. Night."

"Night."

When she crawled into bed half an hour later, Simona still had no idea what to do. She tossed and turned all night and, by morning, was no closer to making a decision. As a result, she was tired and out of sorts. Of course, Yasmine was her usually bubbly self. Outside in the backyard, Simona strapped Yasmine into her swing and pushed gently. The little girl's giggles filled the air.

"I'm glad one of us is happy today," Simona said. "What am I going to do, Yasmine? I promised your mom I'd take care of you, and I plan to do just that. I won't subject you to the same type of scrutiny that followed us back home." Studying her niece's animated face, she said, "I wonder what Donovan would say about you." She sighed heavily and kept up the gentle rhythm of the swing. "I really like Donovan, but I like my privacy, too." She had no idea if he even liked children. "And the man definitely knows how to kiss."

Simona's mind went back to last night's kiss. Each time he kissed her, she lost more and more of her willpower. She glanced down to find Yasmine staring at her and chuckled. "I guess you didn't need to know that bit of information."

Simona stopped the swing and took Yasmine out. Yasmine laid her head on Simona's shoulder. Inhaling her sweet baby scent, Simona smiled. "You're such a precious little one."

But her smile faded quickly. Unless she planned for the barbecue to be her last date with Donovan, she needed to find a way to tell him about her niece. Chances were he wouldn't want to be bothered with a woman who had a child anyway, and he would choose to stop seeing Simona.

Somehow, that thought didn't sit well with her.

Chapter 8

Donovan adjusted the incline on his treadmill and increased his pace, trying to erase the images of himself and Simona naked and writhing in his bed that had plagued him all night long. He had never been so consumed by a woman in his life. He'd thought he was in love with Rolanda, but the emotions rising within him eclipsed those feelings tenfold. And he wasn't sure whether he wanted to embrace them or run like hell.

His mind traveled back to the previous night. He couldn't help but wonder what was going on with Simona. While he would rather not have to deal with the media and general public regularly, she'd appeared almost frightened by the mention of someone taking her picture.

The other thing that crossed his mind was her reluctance to invite him into her house. He hadn't been expecting to take the grand tour when he arrived to pick her up, but he certainly hadn't anticipated her closing and locking the door before he could get a glimpse inside her place.

It was almost as if she was hiding something. Donovan shook off the thought. "Don't go there, man," he muttered breathlessly.

He slowed to a jog and, minutes later, the treadmill stopped. He reached for the towel slung across the top of the machine and wiped the sweat dripping from his face and bare chest.

Once he'd caught his breath, Donovan completed his workout. When he'd purchased the house three years ago, he had one of the five bedrooms converted to a home gym and installed everything he needed to get the same workout as in the high-priced fitness club where he had spent a small fortune. Not only had the equipment already paid for itself, he didn't have to waste time waiting for a particular machine.

Finishing up his workout, Donovan headed to the kitchen for water. He had just taken the first sip when the phone rang. Walking over to a small corner desk, he picked up the handset and checked the display.

"Hey, Mom," he said.

"Hi, Donovan. How are you, honey?"

"I'm good. Are you and Dad okay?" he asked with concern.

"Of course. I just hadn't talked to you in a long time. You usually call me every couple of weeks."

"I know, and I'm sorry. It's been really busy at the office with Terrence out." He took a sip of water. "Janae had the baby a couple of weeks ago."

"Oh, that's wonderful," she gushed. "What did they have?"

"A girl. Nadia Elise Campbell. My little goddaughter is a beauty."

His mother chuckled. "I bet she is. You need to send me some pictures. I bet Terrence has her spoiled rotten already."

Donovan laughed. "He does. He wants to hold her all day, but Janae won't let him."

"Good for her. So, what about you? When are you going to settle down with a nice girl and give me some grand-babies? My neighbor's daughter just had a baby boy. That brings her total to four now. She wanted to know when my children were going to bless me."

Donovan stifled a groan. First Miss Ellie and now his mom. Beverly Wright had been waging this campaign for the past decade, and even more so since Terrence got married.

"What about Giselle?" he asked. His sister was three years younger and had gotten married six months ago. "She's already married. You should be hounding her instead of me."

"As a matter of fact, she and Bryce stopped by last night to tell your father and I that they're expecting their first child. I'm so excited I can hardly stand it," she gushed.

"Wow. I'm happy for them. She didn't call me."

His mother lowered her voice. "She said she was going to call you tonight, so you'd better act surprised. I wasn't supposed to tell, but I couldn't help myself," she added with a giggle.

Donovan laughed heartily. "And *that's* why we don't tell you the things we want kept a secret." He was happy for his sister, but this meant his mother was going to be harassing him more often.

"Oh, boy, hush. Anyway, back to you. You're not getting any younger, Donovan."

"Come on, Mom. Don't start...please."

He heard her deep sigh. "All right. When are you coming to visit? We haven't seen you in almost six months."

"I don't know. It may be a while, but I'll try to get there as soon as I can." His parents had moved from LA to Rockford, Illinois, two years ago to take care of his paternal grandmother. When she died last year, his parents decided to stay. The one good thing was that they were closer to his sister and husband, who lived in Chicago. "How's Dad?"

"He's fine. His blood pressure has stayed down over the past month."

"That's good to hear." His father's blood pressure had been elevated due to the stress of dealing with distant family members challenging his grandmother's will. Thankfully, everything had been resolved, and his father was getting back to his healthy self.

"Well, I know you probably have a lot to do today. Make sure you get some rest. Don't forget to send me the pictures of Terrence's baby. Oh, and don't tell Giselle I told you."

"I won't. Love you, Mom."

"Love you, too, sweetheart. Talk to you soon."

Donovan disconnected and replaced the phone. He couldn't get over the fact that his baby sister was going to be a mom. A wave of loneliness washed over him. He wondered if Simona liked children. At the hospital that first night, he had gotten a glimpse of her thoughtfulness and compassion. Without a doubt, he knew she would make a phenomenal mother.

Shaking his head, he forced the thoughts away. He shouldn't care one way or another. And he shouldn't let her get too close.

Donovan downed the rest of his water and placed the glass in the dishwasher. Not let her get too close? Yeah, right. Something told him he was fighting a losing battle.

Hours later, he sat in his home office getting a few things done for tomorrow. He was meeting with Terrence and Audrey at seven to discuss the employee shift. Stretching, he chuckled, remembering the conversation with his sister. She had known their mother told before he could say anything. And, like his mother, she had asked whether he was seeing someone. Donovan told her about Simona, but reiterated several times that he'd known her only a short time. Her only response had been, "Ooh, I can't wait to tell Mama."

As he leaned back in the chair, a vision of Simona in that blue dress floated through his mind. It had hugged every luscious curve. And those high heels accentuated long, firm legs. His body reacted with lightning speed, and he shifted in the chair. He hadn't been able to stop thinking about that encounter in his office or their last kiss. If he ever got her in his office again, all bets were off. He glanced over at the clock and picked up his cell.

"Hello."

"Hey, beautiful," he said when Simona answered. "Did I catch you at a bad time?"

"No. I'm just putting away some laundry. What's up?"

"Nothing much. I just wanted to hear your sexy voice."

She laughed softly. "I already agreed to go with you to the barbecue, so there's no need to try to butter me up."

"I'm not. You have this low, husky thing going on. It's sexy as hell." When she didn't comment, he spoke her name. "Simona?"

"I'm here. I don't know what to say. No one has ever said that before."

"I'm glad to be the first."

"Donovan, I…"

"What?" he asked when she trailed off.

"I…I was just going to say that you're one of the most thoughtful men I've met."

His gut clenched. "Thanks. You're the first woman who's told me that."

"Well, I'm glad to be the first."

Donovan closed his eyes and tried to force down the emotions swirling in his gut. "So, are you working tomorrow?"

"No. What about you?"

"Yep. I'll probably get to the office around six-thirty."

"That's early. It's after ten, so you should probably get off this phone and go to bed."

"Probably. But what I'd really like to do is come over and kiss you good-night."

"You can get that kiss when I see you next week."

"You don't want me to come over? I promise it'll be worth it."

"I'm sure it will be…next week," Simona said with a laugh.

"Okay, okay." He could listen to her voice all day and night. He sat up abruptly. Where had that thought come from? He was getting way ahead of himself. "I'll call you later this week."

"That's fine. Have a good night."

"You, too." Donovan disconnected, tossed the phone on his desk and drew in a deep breath. Simona was quickly getting under his skin. He had never thought of listening to a woman day and night, yet with her, he would do it in a heartbeat.

On Thursday during her lunch break—the first one she'd had all week—Simona sat with her cell cradled in her palm. She'd had the perfect opportunity to tell Donovan about Yasmine when he called on Sunday, and she'd chickened out. Since then, she had tried to get up the nerve to call him. Here it was, four days later, and she still hadn't said anything, even though she'd had plenty of opportunities. He had called her on Monday, and again last night, and the words stuck in her throat. She had been able to avoid inviting him inside her home so far, but it would be rude not to at least let him get a foot in the door. She was running out of time.

Glancing at the phone in her hand, Simona blew out a long breath. She scrolled through the contacts and found

Donovan's number. Her thumb hovered over the display for several seconds before she changed her mind. Again. She bit into an apple slice.

"Well, if it isn't my favorite nurse. Mind if I join you?"

Simona managed to bite back the retort poised on the tip of her tongue. The last person she wanted to talk to was Lionel Harris. She had managed to dodge him for the past couple of weeks, but it looked as if her luck had run out. She glanced around the cafeteria. There were plenty of empty tables.

"Are you going to make me stand here all day?" he asked, giving her his most charismatic smile. "People are starting to stare."

It would serve him right if she did. "Fine. Sit."

He lowered himself into the chair across from her. "Thanks." He immediately picked up his burger and took a hefty bite.

Simona continued to nibble on her apple slices and waited for him to start in on his campaign. Three…two…one…

"Simona," he started.

Right on cue.

"When are you going to let me take you out to dinner?"

"Never."

"Why? I'm educated and a well-respected physician." He leaned closer and lowered his voice seductively. "And I'm pretty good-looking, if I have to say so myself," he added with a wink.

She sighed heavily. "How many times do I have to tell you no before you stop asking?"

"I can promise you we'll have a good time together," he continued as if she hadn't spoken. "I'll take you to my mountain retreat in Lake Tahoe or my villa in Spain… wherever you want to go."

"The answer is still no, Dr. Harris," Simona said

through clenched teeth. "If you'll excuse me, I need to get back to work." She gathered the remnants of her meal, stood and pasted a smile on her face. "Enjoy your lunch."

Instead of going back to the break room for the last five minutes of her break, she went outside, hoping to cool her temper. Taking a seat on one of the benches, she drew in several deep breaths. Finally her calm returned. Her phone vibrated in her pocket. Frowning, she pulled it out, thinking it was Eve. She was surprised to see a text message from Donovan.

Hey, beautiful. Sitting here thinking about u. Hope ur day is going well. D

No matter how stressful her day was, Donovan always found a way to make her smile. She typed back: Thanks for thinking of me. Hope ur day is going well, too. S

Rising to her feet, Simona went back to the emergency room to finish her shift, praying she could get through the rest of the day without having to deal with Dr. Harris again. On her way, a registration clerk grabbed her arm.

"Can you check on a car outside the front door? I think there's a baby on the way."

Simona gave the clerk some instructions and rushed out the door. By the time she reached the car, a nursing assistant was behind her with supplies. She donned a pair of gloves, quickly wrapped the baby girl who hadn't waited to be born in a hospital, clamped the cord and noted the time for the birth certificate. On the heels of her statement, a gurney arrived. As soon as she got back to the emergency room, a passing doctor asked if she had given a second dose of morphine to the patient in room four. Simona explained that she hadn't logged on to the computer yet, but would do so now and catch up with the orders.

Hours later, Simona dragged herself wearily to her car.

Since that thirty-minute lunch break, the ER had moved nonstop, and she hadn't been able to catch her breath or take a bathroom break. All she wanted to do was go home and fall out, but Simona knew Yasmine would be up for at least an hour, until her bedtime. Before she made it out the door, one of the nurses called to her. She seriously thought about pretending not to hear, but she couldn't do that.

"What do you need, Betty?"

"Nothing. These came for you a few hours ago, but you were so busy I didn't get a chance to tell you." She handed Simona a bouquet of pink roses in a glass vase.

Her eyes narrowed, thinking that Dr. Harris was up to his tricks again. But they were gorgeous. "Thank you. These are lovely." She spied a small white envelope in the center. Simona was anxious to read the card, but didn't want everyone in her business, so she held off.

"Looks like you hit the jackpot. Whoever he is, you'd better hold on to him. I wish some man would give me flowers like that."

"Thanks, Betty. I'll see you tomorrow."

"Okay. Oh, wait. Here's the box so you can bring them in the car."

As soon she was in the driver's seat, Simona plucked the card off and opened it. They were from Donovan.

Because you're you. Donovan

At that moment, she lost a piece of her heart.

She waited until after she had put Yasmine to bed before calling Donovan.

"Yeah," came the clipped greeting when he answered.

"Donovan?"

There was a pause, and then he said, "Simona?"

"Yes, it's me. Am I interrupting?"

"No, no. Sorry about that. I was reading something."

"You're still at work?" she asked incredulously, peeking at her watch. "It's almost ten."

"I know. I'm going home soon."

"You sound exhausted."

"So do you. Long day?"

"Yes. I wanted to thank you for the roses. They're beautiful."

"I'm glad you like them."

"Donovan, I…"

"Did you change your mind about going on Saturday?"

"No, but—"

"But what?"

Simona tightened her grip on the phone, trying to force the words past her constricted throat. What if he decided throwing a child in the mix was too much?

"Simona, are you feeling a little unsure about what's happening between us?"

"A little."

"Sweetheart, I understand where you're coming from, but let's just take things one step at a time. We'll talk more about us on Saturday."

"Okay."

"I need to finish up so I can get out of here."

"Of course. Be careful going home."

"Always."

"Coward," she muttered after disconnecting. Simona knew she was only prolonging the inevitable. Saturday, she told herself. She had to come clean, and hopefully he would understand. What's the worst that could happen?

He could walk away, that nagging voice inside her head reminded her. She didn't think he was that kind of man, but in another week, she would know for sure.

Chapter 9

It had been exactly two weeks since he had seen Simona, and Donovan missed her. Excitement filled him when he pulled into her driveway. The only thing he wanted was to kiss her again. Truth be told, he wanted much more, but he'd settle for the kiss as a start. But he continued to be bothered by their last conversation. She wasn't telling him something. And in the back of his mind, signals flashed, warning him to proceed cautiously. Donovan shoved the warning aside and got out of the car.

When Simona opened the door, his mouth went dry at the sight of her wearing a pair of white shorts, a red sleeveless blouse and low-heeled sandals.

"Hi, Donovan. Come in." Simona stepped back to let him enter.

His brow lifted in surprise. This was the first time she had invited him into her home. "Hey." As soon as they reached the living room, he draped an arm around her waist, lowered his head and kissed her the way he had been dreaming about all week. She captured his tongue and sucked gently. Blood rushed straight to his groin. He pulled her closer, and her soft breasts pressed against his chest, forcing a low moan from his throat. Donovan trailed kisses along her jaw and the scented column of her neck as his fingers deftly unbuttoned her top. "Very sexy," he murmured, transferring his kisses to the exposed portion of her breasts above the black lace bra.

"Donovan," Simona whispered breathlessly.

Donovan reclaimed her mouth once more, then reluctantly lifted his head. If he hadn't promised Terrence and Janae he'd be there today, he would strip Simona slowly and make love to every inch of her sexy body. Not bothering to hide the desire in his eyes, he told her, "We're going to finish this later." He redid her buttons.

"I…I'll be right back." She turned and fled the room.

He was sorely tempted to call Terrence and tell him they'd be late. He wanted Simona…badly…*now*. Donovan scrubbed a hand down his face and tried to get himself under control.

"I'm ready."

He spun around at the sound of Simona's voice. She ran her tongue across her bottom lip, and her gaze drifted to his mouth.

"Baby, don't look at me like that. I promised my friend I'd be at this barbecue, and I'm a man of my word. But if you keep that up, we'll never make it out of here. I won't leave until I know every part of your body inside and out."

Simona gasped. "Um…I wouldn't want you to get in trouble, so we should go."

Donovan glanced around the room once more. "I like your place. It reminds me of you."

"How so?"

"Warm and inviting."

"I think we need to leave." She grabbed him by the hand and dragged him to the front door.

"I'm just saying…"

"Uh-huh. Out. You are too tempting." She locked the door and followed him to the car.

Donovan started the car and turned the air on full blast. Simona laughed. "A little warm?"

His gaze slid over her bare thighs in those shorts and back up to her face. "Blazing." He gripped the steering wheel tighter.

She gave him an amused glance. "Well, let's hope you cool off by the time we get to your friend's house." He grunted, and she laughed harder. "How far is it?"

"About half an hour." He debated telling her just who his "friend" was, but decided to hold off. He wanted Simona to meet Terrence Campbell, not R & B superstar Monte, especially after what happened last weekend at the concert. Donovan didn't buy that she was just camera shy.

They conversed about everything from politics to sports, and he found out that she was a huge NBA fan. When they drove up to the gate, he lowered the window and typed in the code.

"You didn't say we were going to a home that could be featured on *Lifestyles of the Rich and Famous*. I feel way underdressed."

"You look fine. I have on shorts and a T-shirt. Trust me, everybody else will be dressed the same."

He parked in the circle driveway behind Brad's Mercedes, got out and came around to assist her. They skirted the three other cars and walked up three steps to double doors. Donovan rang the bell. While waiting, he observed Simona. She shifted from foot to foot and nibbled on her lip. Before he could comment, the door swung open.

"What's up, D? About time you got here," Terrence said. "And who is this lovely lady?"

"Hey, T. Terrence Campbell, this is Simona Andrews. Simona, Terrence."

"Nice to meet you, Simona," Terrence said. "You guys come on in. Everybody's out back."

Behind Terrence's back, Simona slapped Donovan across the arm and mouthed, "Why didn't you tell me?"

He shrugged and smiled. She rolled her eyes. Holding Simona's hand, they followed Terrence through the house and out to the backyard.

Simona nearly had a heart attack when she realized Donovan's friend was R & B singer and producer Monte. She tried not to stare as they walked through the house, but failed. The tastefully done rooms were the perfect combination of luxury and comfort. But what held her attention were the amazing paintings of landscapes hanging on the walls. She made a mental note to ask Donovan about it later.

As they rounded a corner, a petite woman carrying a very young baby intercepted them. Terrence stopped walking and placed his arm around the woman. "Simona, I'd like you to meet my very beautiful and talented wife, Janae. Janae, this is Simona."

"Nice to meet you, Simona. I'm glad you could make it," Janae said.

"Nice to meet you, too, Janae. Congratulations on the new addition to your family. She's adorable."

"Thank you," Terrence and Janae chorused. The two shared a look of adoration, then Terrence placed a tender kiss on his wife's lips. Simona felt a twinge of jealousy.

"All right, all right, you two. Knock it off. You have guests," Donovan said. "Hey, Janae." He bent to kiss her cheek. "How's my goddaughter doing?" He reached for the baby. "Simona, this little angel is Nadia Elise Campbell."

She smiled at the little bundle. Simona watched in fas-

cination as he gently cradled the baby as if it was second nature. A memory surfaced of the nurse gushing over
Monte being at the hospital. Putting two and two together,
she realized Nadia must have been born the night she met
Donovan.

Outside, Donovan introduced her to several more people, including Janae's parents and Terrence's grandparents.
She found out immediately that what Donovan had told
her about Terrence's grandmother was true. The woman
was a serious matchmaker.

Holding Simona's hands, Mrs. Campbell smiled. "It's
wonderful to meet you, Simona. Call me Miss Ellie or
Grandma."

Donovan stood behind Miss Ellie, frantically shaking
his head and mouthing, "Don't call her Grandma. Don't
do it."

Simona bit her lip to stifle a laugh. When Miss Ellie
turned his way, he quickly composed himself.

"Donovan, she's a lovely girl," Miss Ellie said.

"That she is, Miss Ellie."

Facing Simona again, Miss Ellie asked, "What do you
do?"

"I'm an emergency room nurse."

"*Really?*" A huge grin blossomed on the woman's face,
and Simona felt the urge to flee.

"Grandma, are you over here trying to play matchmaker
again?" Terrence asked, placing an arm around his grandmother's shoulders and winking at Simona. "Simona, you'll
have to excuse my grandmother." He kissed the elderly
woman on the cheek. "Come on, Grandma. Stop scaring
Simona, or she won't want to come back." He led her away.

When they were out of earshot, Simona said, "She is
scary."

Donovan laughed and placed a quick kiss on her lips.
"I told you."

* * *

Later, after mingling and consuming too much food, Simona sought out a lounger and collapsed. She hadn't known what to expect when she arrived, but had found everyone to be friendly and unpretentious. Her gaze strayed to Donovan sitting in a chair holding Nadia. He seemed to love children, which gave her hope. Yasmine would celebrate her first birthday next weekend, and if things went well, maybe she would introduce Donovan then.

Earlier, Eve had taken Yasmine to her house so they wouldn't be home when Donovan arrived. Simona had checked and triple checked to make sure all evidence of a baby in her living room was gone. A measure of guilt rose up, but she pushed it back down. She was just trying to protect her niece, she reasoned.

She had no idea how long she lay there with her eyes closed until Donovan's voice filtered through her haze.

"Hey, sleepyhead. You all right?" He took a seat on the edge of the lounger.

Opening her eyes, she smiled. "Yeah. I guess I was a little tired and I ate too much," she added with a chuckle. "It was a long week."

He stood and extended his hand. "Come dance with me."

"Dance?" Only then did she hear the music and see the couples—Terrence and Janae, Janae's best friend, Karen, and her husband, Damian, and Terrence's grandparents—swaying to the slow tune being filtered through hidden speakers.

She stood, and he led her over to where everyone danced. After what happened in her house this afternoon, Simona wasn't sure she could take being in his arms for any length of time. He'd had every molecule in her body electrified.

Now he wrapped his arms around her and started a

slow grind that made her nipples hard and her center throb. Donovan stared down at her with those magnetic eyes, communicating exactly what he meant, and she had no problem interpreting the message.

"I love holding your body close to mine," he whispered in her ear. "I can't wait to have you in my bed. You have to feel what you do to me."

A soft gasp escaped when she felt the solid bulge of his erection pressing against her lower belly. A shudder passed through her, and she missed a step. His gaze never left hers as one arm held her closer while his other hand burned a path down her back and caressed her hip. All Simona wanted was for him to find a bed and finish what he'd started.

Donovan's brow lifted, and a wicked smile curved his mouth. "Don't tempt me, sweetheart."

Her eyes widened. There was no way he could know what she was thinking. Could he? She was almost afraid to ask. "What do you mean?"

"You're thinking we need to find the nearest bed and finish this."

"How…how did you…?"

"Your eyes tell me everything I need to know." He nibbled on her bottom lip, teased the corners with his tongue and plunged inside when she parted her lips.

Her eyes slid closed. Where in the world did he learn to kiss like this? Almost immediately, sanity returned and she remembered where they were. She pushed against his chest and broke off the kiss. "Donovan, did you forget we're standing in a backyard full of people?" she whispered.

"Nope. Believe me, those men are so in love with their wives they aren't paying attention to us. Take a look."

Simona risked a peek over her shoulder and saw that what Donovan said was true. The couples were totally into each other. But still…

"See," he said, gifting her with tender kisses along her jaw and lips.

She was glad when the song ended because she needed to go somewhere and get herself together. "Do you know where the bathroom is?"

Donovan smiled knowingly, nodded and directed her inside to a cabana-like room.

As soon as she closed the door, Simona fell against it and tried to slow her heart rate. She had never had a man seduce her the way Donovan was doing, and she didn't think she could take much more before succumbing to the pleasure he was sure to give her.

After a few moments, she felt in control enough to re-join the party. Back outside, Simona noticed that the guys had moved to one side of the yard while the ladies all sat around on the other side. Janae's parents and Terrence's grandparents were nowhere in sight. She guessed they might have gone inside.

"Simona, come join us," Janae called out, waving her over. When Simona sat in a vacant chair, Janae said, "We haven't had a chance to get acquainted. So, how did you and Donovan meet?"

Simona stared at the smiling faces of the three women. Aside from Eve, she hadn't developed any real friendships since coming to LA. "I was getting off work in the emergency room and wasn't watching where I was going. Next thing I know I'm being saved from a coffee cart running me over. Coming here today, I realize it was the night Nadia was born. I think Donovan was leaving the hospital."

"Aw, that's so sweet. Donovan's such a nice guy," Karen said.

"I've known him since college, and I agree wholeheart-edly," Audrey added. Simona found out that Audrey and

Brad married after college, and also that they headed up
departments at the recording company.

"If you don't mind me asking, Janae, how did you and
Terrence meet?" She was curious how Janae handled her
husband's fame.

"I don't mind at all. This one here," she started, ges-
turing toward Karen, "dragged me to his concert in San
Francisco two years ago. We were instantly attracted to
each other, but I had no intentions of dating someone as
famous as he is. But my ever-resourceful husband enlisted
the help of his best friend over there—" she pointed at
Donovan "—and tricked us into coming backstage after
the concert."

"Girl, there was so much heat between them that I had
to give them a minute alone," Karen interrupted, fanning
herself. They all laughed.

"Whatever," Janae said, rolling her eyes. "*Anyway*, Simona, to make a long story short, we dated long-distance
for a while—I was a special education teacher in San
Jose—and moved here when we married."

"Doesn't it bother you, having all the media in your
business?" Simona asked.

"I don't like the spotlight at all, but Terrence is very pro-
tective of his family and he does a great job keeping our
private lives *private*. The one time a reporter tried to stir
up some trouble, I saw a side of my husband I didn't know
existed. Suffice it to say we haven't had any more problems. Ask Donovan. As Terrence's agent-slash-manager,
he held a nice little press conference."

Her eyes widened. *Agent?* That meant he was more vis-
ible than she thought. She groaned inwardly. One more
thing to add to her growing list of worries. Simona thought
about her own experience with the media and the stark
contrast in how her situation was handled. Would Donovan be the same? And could she risk it? Memories of that

time flooded her mind—cameras following her everywhere, waiting at her home and job. She glanced over at Donovan laughing. As much as she enjoyed being with him, she didn't think she'd be able to let go of her hang-ups.

The women's laughter brought her back to the conversation.

"Shoot, you should be thanking me, Janae," Karen was saying.

"That goes both ways, missy," Janae shot back. "If you hadn't come to my wedding on the cruise, you wouldn't have met your husband."

Simona stared curiously.

"Amen, girl!" Karen said, lifting her hand to high-five Janae. To Simona she said, "Damian was on the cruise with a couple of his friends, and I was taking a dating hiatus. The moment I saw him, I forgot all about that hiatus."

Simona laughed. "I can see why. He is a good-looking man." With his towering height, golden-brown skin and hazel eyes, Damian Bradshaw could fuel the fantasies of most women.

Audrey sighed dramatically. "I'm the only one who doesn't have a fabulous story to tell. We met in college, dated for four years and got married. No fuss, no cruise ships, concerts or knight-in-shining-armor saves."

Laughing, Janae said, "Maybe, but you still have a true love story. You guys have been married for almost ten years, and together longer than that."

A smile played around Audrey's mouth. "Yeah, you have a point."

The women shared a smile and a moment of quiet reflection before resuming the conversation. Simona enjoyed the camaraderie she was building with these women. Her cell phone rang and she answered, still smiling.

"Hey, Simona."

"Hey, Eve."

"Sorry to bother you, but I thought you'd want to know that Yasmine is running a fever and she's not keeping any food down. A couple of hours ago her temperature was one hundred and two point seven. I gave her the Tylenol, and she promptly threw it back up. I tried the Pedialyte, and she's not keeping that down, either."

Panic arose in Simona. "What's her temperature now?"

"It's almost a hundred and four, and she's pretty listless, poor thing."

She was on her feet. "Try a cool bath, and I'll be there as soon as I can." She disconnected and took in the concerned gazes of the other women. "I'm sorry. I have an emergency and I have to leave."

They all stood and Janae said, "Is there anything we can do?" When Simona shook her head, she said, "Okay, but make sure you let us know that everything is all right."

"I will." She caught Donovan's gaze. Evidently he knew something was wrong because he was up and striding across the yard.

Time had run out. She should have told him about Yasmine. This wasn't the way she wanted him to find out, and now she didn't have a choice. She could only pray that he would understand.

Chapter 10

Donovan half listened to Terrence as he stole glances at Simona sitting across the yard talking with Janae, Karen and Audrey. She fit in well, if all the laughter was an indication. But then, with her personality, he'd known she would. The other thing he was starting to realize was that she fit well with him, too. As much as he wanted to keep her at a distance, he couldn't.

"Donovan, are you listening?" Terrence asked.

"What?"

Damian and Brad laughed.

Terrence shook his head. "Man, can you stop staring at your woman for five minutes? I said I'll be in the office a couple of days next week and wanted to know if you're going to Chicago with Kaleidoscope next weekend."

"I hadn't planned on it, since you've been out. Are you going to be back by then?"

"I don't know. Don't forget I have to do the music class."

"Oh, yeah." His attention shifted back to Simona.

"Donovan, maybe you should just go over there. Obviously, we're not interesting enough," Damian said.

Terrence chuckled. "Looks like you're gonna be the next to fall, D. Simona seems really nice."

"She is," Donovan said absently.

"Take it from a group of happily married men—don't let a good woman get away."

Brad and Damian lifted their cups in mock salute.

"Tell it!"

"Preach, brother!"

Suddenly, Simona shot up off her chair with a cell phone to her ear, preempting anything Donovan planned to say. Her panic-stricken gaze propelled him to his feet and across the yard in a few strides. "What's the matter, baby?"

"I…I have to go. My neighbor called and…there's an emergency."

"Is it your house?" She shook her head quickly. "What is it?"

"It's my…it's…" She swiped at the tears filling her eyes.

Donovan's heart nearly stopped. He gathered her in his arms. "It's okay. Let's go." They said their goodbyes and rushed to his car.

"We should be there in about thirty minutes," she was saying on the phone as they drove out of the gates.

Throughout the drive, she didn't talk, but he caught glimpses of her wiping her face. She hadn't told him what was going on, and all kinds of scenarios crossed his mind. Every time he tried to ask her, the tears would start, so he stopped asking. By the time he made it to her house, his nerves were stretched tight. She practically jumped out of the car before he could put it in park. He climbed out and quickly caught up with her.

The sight that greeted him when she opened the door rendered him mute. A tall, attractive woman emerged carrying a baby girl who resembled Simona and who looked to be less than a year old. His heart lurched, and his gut clenched. *She has a baby? Why didn't she tell me?* His mind was bombarded with a thousand and one questions.

"Hey, sweet pea," Simona said, reaching for the baby. "Has her fever gone down at all, Eve?" she asked with concern.

"No," the woman answered. "And she still can't keep anything down."

Simona placed a kiss on the baby's brow. "I think I'd better take her in to emergency. It's probably a virus, but with her history, I don't want to take any chances." She finally turned to Donovan. "I'm sorry." Something like regret flickered in her gaze.

The woman, whom he assumed was her neighbor, said, "Simona, I'll go and fix a couple of bottles." She divided a wary glance between Donovan and Simona and walked out.

Simona nibbled on her lip, something he realized she did as a nervous habit. "I need to pack her bag, but…"

"Go pack the bag. I'll take her." Donovan gently took the baby from her arms.

"Um…she doesn't really do well with strangers."

He glared at her. "Go pack the bag, Simona," he said softly.

She nodded, turned and took off down the hall.

"Simona?"

She paused.

"What's her name?"

"Yasmine."

Donovan stared down at the little girl. Even though he hadn't spent much time around small babies, he knew Yasmine didn't feel well. Her eyes were glassy, and her cheeks were reddened. She stared up at him, scrunched her face as if she was about to cry then relaxed her features. She lifted her small hand, touched his face and placed her head against his chest. A myriad of emotions filled his heart and he fell...*hard*.

"Hey, Yasmine." He used his thumb to wipe the moisture around her temple. "You're going to be just fine, angel." He spun around at the sound of Simona's voice.

"Okay. I'm ready." She accepted the bottles from her friend and added them to the bag. Simona walked over to where Donovan stood holding Yasmine and put a jacket on her.

Donovan handed her the baby. "I'll drive you."

Her eyes widened. "We'll be fine," she said quickly.

"You're in no shape to drive, and Yasmine might need you with her," he argued.

"Eve was going to go with me."

He could tell Simona didn't want to be alone with him. And with good reason.

"Ah, Simona. You go ahead with him. Call me later." The woman walked over and extended her hand to Donovan. "I'm Eve Thompson, Simona's neighbor. You must be Donovan. It's nice to finally meet you."

He stared at her questioningly and shook her hand. "Donovan Wright. Same here."

"I'll see you later, Simona." Eve gathered up some papers and stuffed them in a bag.

Donovan gestured toward the door. "Let's go." He took a few moments to transfer the car seat and make sure they were buckled in before leaving. They completed the drive in total silence, except for the two times he heard Simona talking to Yasmine. Trust and honesty were the two things that topped his list, and he never would have expected her to keep something like this from him. More questions invaded his thoughts. Had she been married before? And *where was Yasmine's father*? The fact that she hadn't trusted him enough made his chest tighten and angered him further. He took several deep breaths and let them out slowly in the hopes it would ease the tension.

By the time they reached the hospital, he had found a small measure of calm. Luckily, because it was only five-thirty in the evening, the emergency room wasn't crowded. They were called within twenty minutes. Common sense and anger dictated that he stay in the waiting room—after all, he wasn't the father—but he couldn't do it. Little Yasmine had tugged on his heart the moment she touched him. Donovan and Simona still hadn't exchanged any words outside of what was absolutely necessary, but he followed them back.

Donovan listened and found out that Yasmine had been born early and had been on a ventilator for two weeks following her birth. The doctor examined her and concluded that she had a virus. But because she was unable to keep anything down, including the fever-reducing medication, the doctor prescribed a suppository, as he wanted to keep her fever from climbing any higher. Donovan tried to stay out of the way, but every time he moved, Yasmine's eyes would follow him.

After an hour, he couldn't take it. That little angelic face and sad eyes pushed him over the edge. Donovan crossed the room to where she lay, stroked her forehead placed a kiss there. "How're you feeling, sweetheart? You don't feel as warm." When he held her hand, tiny fingers wrapped around his pinky, drawing him in even more.

"She's really taking to you," Simona said. "I've never seen her do that with anyone."

There was a lot he wanted to say, but the words stuck in his throat. Instead he just shrugged.

It took another two hours for the fever to break, after which Yasmine was able to keep down a small amount of liquid and was released to go home. Donovan carried the sleeping baby into the house while Simona removed the car seat.

"Let me go put her to bed."

Donovan kissed Yasmine once more and handed her over to Simona, staring after her as she walked down a hallway. He dropped wearily onto the loveseat and braced his head in his hands. He'd thought he finally found a woman he could trust and who would trust him.

"Donovan?"

His head came up slowly. "I guess I know now why you never invited me into your house. So, when were you going to tell me?"

Simona wrung her hands. "I don't know."

"Simona, we've been going out for almost a month."

"I know and I tried to tell—"

He jumped to his feet and cut her off. "When? We've talked on the phone several times. Not once did you mention that you have a child!"

She ran a hand across her forehead. "Donovan, you have to understand. I was just trying to protect her."

"Protect her?" he yelled. Remembering Yasmine was asleep, he clenched his teeth and lowered his voice. "From what? Who?"

"Yes, protect her. I didn't want to start bringing strange men around her."

"So, that's what I am, huh? A strange man." He chuckled mirthlessly. "Thanks for letting me know where I stand." He stalked to the door with her following closely on his heels.

"No. Donovan, wait. That's not what I meant."

He regarded her thoughtfully. "No? So, what...next you're gonna tell me you have a husband hidden away somewhere?" He shook his head. "I hoped we had something special, but now I don't know what to believe. See you around." Donovan closed the door behind him without waiting for a response.

Ten minutes into his drive, he realized he had been going at least twenty miles per hour above the speed limit and eased off the gas. The last thing he needed in his present mood was a speeding ticket. Coming to a stoplight, he briefly closed his eyes.

Why are you so upset, Wright? Opening them again, he slammed his hand against the steering wheel and cursed under his breath. He didn't have to search very far for the answer. There was only one reason why he would be this angry. Somehow Simona had gotten to him. Despite all his big talk of keeping a woman at arm's length, she had managed to wiggle her way under his skin.

Simona stood staring at the space that Donovan had vacated. How could a day that started with so much promise end in such disaster? A vision of his shocked and angry expression continued to play in her mind, and the hurt in his voice caused a knot to form in her belly. She closed her eyes and rubbed her temples, feeling the beginnings of a headache.

Walking across the room, she slowly lowered herself onto the sofa and laid her head against the back. She berated herself over and over. Why hadn't she told him? Donovan was right. They'd been seeing each other for a month, and she'd had plenty of opportunities. But he hadn't even given her a chance to explain before he stormed out. And that pissed her off. *Nothing I can do about it tonight.*

Rising, she checked on Yasmine and gently touched her skin. Although she was still warm, Simona was relieved to find that the fever hadn't risen. The doorbell rang as she exited the baby's room. Thinking Donovan had returned, she quickened her steps. She opened the door to find Eve, not Donovan, standing there and tried to hide her disappointment. Simona stepped back to let her enter.

"How's Yasmine?"

"The doctor thinks she has a virus. We got the fever down, and she was able to keep a couple ounces of the Pedialyte down."

"And Donovan?"

Simona shook her head. "He's really angry. He didn't even give me a chance to say anything." Tears welled in her eyes. "All I wanted was to protect my niece. I still have concerns about his job, and even more after today's barbecue. You'll never guess who his 'friend' is."

"Who?"

"Monte."

"As in, the fine R & B singer with that sexy, deep voice?"

"The one and only."

"So were there fans and groupies there?"

"No. Just his family and close friends. And they all called him Terrence. His wife is really nice."

"So, help me out here—what exactly are you still concerned about? It seems as though Donovan has gone out of his way to show you that he's just a regular guy who happens to have a job that requires him to make public appearances."

"He's more than the vice president of the company. He's Monte's agent, manager, or whatever you want to call it, as well as another one of the label's artists."

"And your point would be? Never mind. Don't answer. Simona, stop using Yasmine as an excuse not to get close to Donovan. Honey, you can't keep comparing him to your ex."

"I know, and I'm trying. But every time I think about what happened, it scares me to death. You have no idea how it feels to have cameras shoved in your face all the time."

"You're right, I don't. And I don't want to," Eve added. "But if you told Donovan, I think he'd understand."

"It's probably too late now," Simona said with a weary sigh. Up to this point, she hadn't realized how much she liked being with Donovan.

"Girl, please. He'll be back. He was just shell-shocked."

"I don't think so. You didn't see him. Anyway, it's probably better this way." She said the words, but she knew they were far from the truth. She didn't feel better. Not wanting to continue down the road to misery, she asked, "Do you think we should cancel the party next Saturday?" For Yasmine's birthday she had invited Eve's five-year-old niece and two-year-old twin nephews over for a small celebration.

"She should be fine by then, and the kids are looking forward to coming." Eve checked her watch. "I need to do some studying. Hang in there, and call me if you need something. The party's at eleven, right?"

Simona nodded. "Yes, I figure they can play, have lunch and cake, then be ready for naps." She hugged her friend. "Thanks for everything, Eve."

Contrary to what Eve believed, Donovan didn't come back. Along with her grueling work days the following week, Simona's nights were filled with thoughts of Donovan—his touch, his kiss, his random text messages asking about her day, and his low, sexy voice that always heated her insides.

She had called and left messages for him twice earlier in the week, and he never responded. On Thursday after work, she picked up the phone and tried again. She was so shocked that he answered the phone that she was momentarily stunned. Recovering her voice, she said, "Donovan, it's Simona."

"What can I do for you?"

His curt reply stung, but she plowed on. "I wanted to explain about Yasmine."

Donovan chuckled bitterly. "Oh, so now you want to talk. I think it's a little late for that."

Simona sighed deeply. "I know I should have told you."

"Yeah, you should have told me. I need to get back to work. Is there anything else?"

"No," she said softly.

"Goodbye, Simona."

She hung up and dropped the cordless back in the base. "I guess that's that," she said miserably.

By Saturday, she was too tired to celebrate anything. But she forced herself to get moving. Yasmine was back to her usually happy self, and her appetite had returned. *At least there's one thing going well right now,* Simona mused. What about the other parts of her life? Though she had known him only a short time, she missed Donovan more than she imagined. She tried to convince herself that it would be better this way, that he'd only disrupt her quiet life.

There was only one problem with her theory: since meeting him, Simona had been happier than she could remember in a long time. And she wasn't sure if the solitary life she had envisioned when she relocated a year ago was the one she wanted now.

Chapter 11

"You've been sulking all week," Terrence said without preamble, pushing his way into the house when Donovan opened the door.

Donovan expelled a harsh breath, closed the door and went into the family room, where Terrence was already sprawled out on the sofa.

"What's going on? I've been trying to catch up with you for days."

"I've been busy. Remember, I'm the only one in the office."

Terrence cut him a look. "Look, D, instead of spending Friday night with my two favorite girls, my wife sent me over here to find out what happened with Simona. She likes her a lot and is concerned. As a matter of fact, so is Audrey. Oh, and did I mention Karen called yesterday to ask about her? So is she all right?"

Dropping into a chair, Donovan scowled at Terrence. He didn't want to have this conversation tonight...or any night, for that matter. He had spent the entire week trying to erase Simona from his thoughts and had failed miserably.

"And Janae told me to get Simona's phone number. She wants to call herself."

His scowl deepened.

"You might as well talk, because I was instructed not to leave without answers. So what was the emergency?"

He groaned. That sounded just like Janae. He and Terrence engaged in a stare down for several seconds before Donovan said, "Her eleven-month-old daughter was sick, and we had to take her to emergency."

Terrence's face registered shock. "Daughter? She has a daughter?"

"Yeah."

"Is she okay?"

He shrugged. "Far as I know." All week, he had been tempted to call or go over to check on the little girl, but his anger far outweighed his concern. He wanted to ask about her when Simona called yesterday, but just hearing Simona's voice stirred up all the mistrust again, and he'd ended the call as quickly as he could.

"What do you mean, 'far as I know'? You haven't talked to Simona?"

"She called last night, but there's nothing to talk about. She lied to me, T. Do you know how I felt walking into that house and seeing that little girl? I thought she was different, but I guess I was wrong. For all I know, she could be married." Even as he said the words, he couldn't believe Simona would do something like that.

"Come off it, Donovan. You know damn well she's not married. She doesn't strike me as a person who would date one man while being married to another. I'm sure she had a good reason as to why she hadn't mentioned it yet."

"I wouldn't know," he grumbled. "I didn't stick around to find out."

Terrence shook his head slowly. "I can't believe you acted a complete idiot. You're behaving worse than I did with Janae."

Donovan stared at his shoes and remained silent.

"You know I'm right."

So what if he was right? He looked up when Terrence laughed. "What's so funny?"

"You. With all the grief you gave me when I was fighting my feelings for Janae, I figured you'd have your stuff together once you met the right woman."

"What makes you think she's the right woman?"

"If she wasn't, you wouldn't be this upset. You'd move on without a backward glance." Terrence stood and pulled out his phone. "I'm going home to my amazing wife and daughter. What's Simona's number?" When Donovan hesitated, he added, "You can give it to me, or I can have Janae, or worse, Audrey, get it."

Donovan cursed under his breath and tossed Terrence the phone.

Terrence chuckled. "Yeah. That's what I thought." He input the information, handed the phone back and headed toward the front door.

Donovan rose to his feet, pocketed the phone and followed.

"We've been friends for a long time, D, and you, better than anybody else, know my history. I never thought I'd fall in love, but I gotta tell you, meeting and falling in love with Janae has been the best thing that's ever happened to me. Going home and knowing that she and Nadia are there gives a new meaning to *home*. I hope Simona's daughter is all right, and you should check on her. Let me know if there's anything I can do. I'll be in the office on Monday."

They shared a rough hug. "Tell Janae hi, and kiss Nadia for me." Donovan closed the door behind his friend and leaned his head against it. Trust meant everything to him, and Simona broke that trust. He couldn't be with a woman he didn't trust.

Then why couldn't he stop thinking about Simona? Or Yasmine? His heart clenched with the remembrance of the little girl reaching up to touch his face then laying her head on his chest, and her tiny hand clutching his finger.

Going upstairs to his bedroom, he flopped down on the bed. As much as he hated to admit it, Terrence was right. Donovan had never had a problem moving on from a woman, which forced him to stop and analyze his feelings for Simona. What he felt for her went beyond mere *liking*. He didn't know how it happened, but in the short month that he'd known her, she had touched a part of his heart that no other woman had before, including Rolanda. Yes, he'd had strong feelings for Rolanda, they got along well and were comfortable with each other, but he held no illusions of a deep, abiding love—the kind he saw with his parents, Terrence and Janae, or Terrence's grandparents.

Simona was a different story. With her, he wanted more, and it scared him. If he were really honest with himself, he would admit to being a little jealous of the fact that she'd had a child with some other man. A man who, evidently, wasn't owning up to his responsibilities. He frowned. Who was this guy, and more importantly, *where* was he? Donovan shook his head. Why did he even care?

He showered and crawled into bed, preparing himself for what he knew would be another sleepless night. He tossed and turned, dreaming about Simona and all the ways and places they could make love. He woke up hot and hard. Groaning, Donovan threw the covers off and stomped downstairs to his gym to work off his sexual frustration.

Two hours later, his body was under control, but his mind continued to race. Making a decision, he quickly downed a protein shake and went up to shower.

* * *

Before he could talk himself out of going over, Donovan hopped in his car and drove off. The closer he came to Simona's house, the faster his heart thumped in his chest. What was wrong with him? Donovan parked in the driveway behind Simona's Honda and was curious about the other cars in the driveway and in front of her house. *You're just here to check on the baby, Wright. Nothing more.* He steeled himself and knocked on the door.

"Donovan! Um…hi," Simona said when she opened the door, clearly surprised.

He shoved his hands in his pockets to keep from hauling her into his arms and kissing her senseless. Her braids hung loose, spilling around her shoulders and down her back, and she had on a pair of shorts and a tank top that left her smooth, toned coffee-with-cream skin bare, sorely tempting him to explore every inch. "Hey."

She eyed him warily and stepped back. "Come in."

He had only planned to ask about Yasmine and leave, but his feet missed that memo and propelled him across her threshold. She closed the door and stood with her arms folded. His gaze zeroed in on her biting her bottom lip, and he wanted to soothe the spot with his tongue and…

Shaking himself mentally, he lifted his eyes back to hers. "I wanted to see how Yasmine is doing." He heard voices and laughter coming from the back of the house. "Oh, I'm sorry. I didn't realize you had company. I'll just come back another time." He turned to the door.

Simona caught his arm. "You don't have to leave. Yesterday was Yasmine's first birthday, so we're having a little party. Why don't you come see for yourself how she's doing?"

Was Yasmine's father here? And did Donovan really want to know? Curiosity got the best of him…and he wanted to see the baby. He nodded. "Okay. Just for a minute." She gave him a soft smile and his heart skipped a beat, reminding him how much he missed seeing that smile. Then he remembered her deceit.

He followed through the living room and moderately sized kitchen to the sliding glass door that led to the backyard. He saw Eve talking with two couples, as a girl about five or six, two younger boys who looked to be twins and Yasmine sat on a nearby blanket playing with toys. All eyes turned his way, and Eve smiled. Simona made introductions to Eve's two younger sisters and their husbands. He didn't want to examine the relief he felt upon finding out that neither of the men present was Yasmine's father.

"She looks like she recovered well," Donovan said, watching Yasmine bang on a toy that lit up and played music.

"She did."

He was itching to go over and pick her up, and Simona must have realized it.

"You can go over if you want."

He slowly approached, and all four children turned his way. Donovan squatted down next to the beautiful little girl, marveling at the difference between the first time he'd seen her and now. Her big brown eyes were bright, and she babbled happily. When she looked up at him, she paused and stuck her lip out as if she would start crying at any moment.

Donovan smiled. "Hey, angel. So now that you're feeling better, you're going to cry?"

Yasmine stared at him for a long moment, seemingly trying to decide. Finally, she pushed herself up to a standing position and gave him a huge grin, showing off a mouth full of tiny teeth and stealing another piece of his heart. Unable to resist, he picked her up and kissed her forehead. "I'm glad you're feeling better." She patted his cheeks and babbled something. Donovan laughed. "Really? All that, huh?" He picked up the toy she had been playing with. "Make some music for me, baby girl." She started banging on the buttons again, the sound warming his soul.

Simona stood off to the side, watching Donovan. She didn't know which look she liked more, his usual business wear or the basketball shorts and T-shirt he had on now. The sight of his lean, muscular build, tight butt and strong calves made her mouth water. Her gaze was drawn to his smile as he interacted with Yasmine, who laughed at whatever he was saying. She had never seen the little girl take to anyone so quickly. Simona sighed inwardly. Seeing him again was hard, especially since he had clearly only come to check on her niece. He hadn't kissed Simona, hugged her or even touched her.

Eve came and stood next to her. "I told you he'd be back."

"He only came back to check on Yasmine. He's barely even talked to me."

"Doesn't matter. He could've easily called or sent a text. He would've never come here if he didn't feel something for you."

"Simona, who is that fine man?" Eve's sister Joanna asked.

"He's a friend."

"Friend? Girl, you do *not* friend zone a man like that. Nah. With a man like him, you drag him to the nearest empty room, rip his clothes off and have your way with him."

"Is that right?" a male voice drawled behind them.

Simona, Eve and Joanna spun around to see Joanna's husband standing there, glaring, with his arms folded. Simona and Eve shared a look and tried to keep from laughing.

Joanna leaned up and kissed her husband. "Yep, just

like I do to you, baby. I think I need something to drink."
She hurried off with him trailing her.

Simona and Eve burst out laughing. Simona said, "Your
sister is a hot mess."

"That she is," Eve agreed. "Always has been. But she
does have a point. Ain't nothing sexier than a fine man
playing with a baby."

Simona grudgingly conceded the point. She observed
as the twins vied for Donovan's attention. He sat on the
blanket, and they climbed onto his lap. He made room for
them, but never put Yasmine down. As if sensing her pe-
rusal, he turned toward Simona. Their eyes locked, but his
expression was unreadable. He turned away when Yasmine pulled on his lips. Simona's eyes slid closed with the
memory of those same lips pressed against hers, moving
slowly down her neck and over the tops of her breasts…

"Simona."

She jumped, and her eyes popped open. Donovan stood
in front of her. "I'm sorry, did you say something?" She
had been so lost in her fantasy that she hadn't heard him
approach. Heat filled her face.

"Yeah. I'm getting ready to leave. I'm glad she's doing
well." An awkward silence settled between them.

"Oh, okay. Well, thanks for stopping by. Are you sure
you don't want to stay for cake?"

He shook his head quickly. "No. Thanks. I have some
stuff to take care of."

She nodded, waiting for him to say something, anything about them.

"Simona, I—"

He bent and scooped up Yasmine, who had toddled over
and grabbed his leg. *Great timing.*

"I have to go, angel. You be a good girl, okay?" He caressed her back and kissed her cheek, then handed her to

Simona. "You don't have to walk me out. I can find my way." He paused a beat. "I'll see you later."

He pivoted and sauntered off, leaving Simona to stare at his retreating back. She tickled Yasmine. "Thanks a lot, little one. Your timing is rotten. Come on, let's go cut your cake."

An hour later, she said goodbye to her guests and laid the sleeping birthday girl in her crib. Eve had helped with most of the cleanup, so Simona washed the few remaining dishes then went to put her feet up. Almost immediately, an image of Donovan drifted through her mind. A smile formed on her lips as she recalled him playing with the kids, and she knew instinctively he would make a terrific father someday.

Her thoughts shifted to Joanna's comments. The moment she'd seen him standing outside her front door, Simona had wanted to do exactly that—drag him to her bedroom, strip him naked and run her hands all over his hard body. She wanted to feel his hands on her, too, to put out the fire that had been building from the first time they kissed. Heated memories surfaced, and an involuntary moan slipped from her mouth. She clenched her fists to stop the sensations from flaring to life.

His visit had taken her completely by surprise, and she wished their conversation hadn't been interrupted. Was he planning to break things off? Her stomach dropped at that thought, although she kept telling herself it was for the best. But what did she really want? Her emotions were all over the place, and she was more confused than ever. One way or another, they needed to talk. She couldn't go through another tortuous week like the past one.

Chapter 12

Donovan rushed around his room packing. He tossed underwear and socks into his bag, added shorts, a T-shirt, tennis shoes and his toiletries. Taking a quick peek at his watch, he zipped the duffel and his garment bag. His plane would be leaving in ninety minutes. Barring any traffic, he should get to the airport in twenty minutes. He hadn't expected the range of emotions that had consumed him when he saw Simona and Yasmine, and he needed some distance. He loped down the stairs, locked up and hopped in the car.

By the time he made it to Chicago, Kaleidoscope's concert would be just starting. He would miss the first half of the show, but catch the entire second one on Sunday. He got to the airport, parked and made it through security just as boarding began. When he was settled in his seat, he pulled out his cell.

"Hey, T," he said when Terrence answered.

"Hey. How's Simona and her daughter?"

"They're fine, but I'm not calling about that. I wanted to let you know I'm flying to Chicago for Kaleidoscope's concerts, and I'll be back Monday night."

There was a pause before Terrence said, "I thought you were having Nigel and Joy travel for the Detroit, Chicago and Philadelphia shows."

"They are. I just thought I'd go to make sure things are going as scheduled."

"Have they had problems, and when did you decide to do this?"

"No, and today."

"Then…"

"Like I said, I'm just checking on things. See you when I get back." Donovan disconnected without giving Terrence a chance to reply. They had been friends since high school and were as close as brothers, so had that conversation gone one minute longer, Terrence would have figured out the real reason for this impromptu flight. He wasn't ready to explain to Terrence, or himself, for that matter, why he felt the need to run halfway across the country instead of facing his dilemma head-on.

When the plane landed, Donovan grabbed his bags, picked up his rental and programmed the House of Blues address into the GPS. He was tired and his mind was still in turmoil, but he was glad to have some space between him and Simona so he could think. Being close to her challenged his resolve to remain distant, in ways he never anticipated.

He was lucky enough to find parking in one of the nearby garages, and the concert was in full swing when he entered. Donovan had taken the time to call Joy to let her know he would be there to avoid him having problems getting into the club.

"Hey, Donovan," Joy said, greeting him with a hug. "We

didn't expect you, but I'm always glad to see you, boss," she added with a smile.

He chuckled. "I thought I'd come and make sure you guys weren't having any problems." Truthfully, he had missed this aspect of his job.

"The shows went great in Detroit, and we sold out both shows tonight and tomorrow night."

"Sounds good. We can talk more later." Joy went back to her duties, and Donovan leaned against the wall to listen to the show. Usually listening to music relaxed him, but tonight it didn't work. He suspected nothing would work except being honest with himself. Not tonight, he decided. Maybe tomorrow.

After the show, he turned on his cell and found that Terrence had sent him a text: Simona got to u, and ur running... ROFL! Donovan muttered a curse and deleted the message, not bothering to respond. Instead, he dialed his sister's number.

"Hey, Giselle."

"Donovan! This is a surprise. I never talk to you twice in a week."

"Yeah, and whose fault is that? Since you married Bryce, you kicked me to the curb," he said with mock sadness.

She laughed. "Wow, that's a low blow. So, to what do I owe this honor?"

"You up for a visit from your big brother?"

"I'd love for you to visit. It's been almost six months. When are you coming?"

"About twenty minutes," he said with a chuckle.

"Wait! You're here? Now?"

"Yep."

"You didn't tell me you were coming when we talked a week ago."

"I didn't know then."

"Oo-kay. Hmm, interesting."

"Kaleidoscope is at the House of Blues tonight and tomorrow, and since I *am* their manager, it shouldn't be a surprise that I'd be here."

"Uh-huh. You're staying the night, aren't you? You'd better not be staying in a hotel. You need directions?"

"Nope. I'll just plug the address into the GPS."

"You hungry?"

"Starved." He hadn't eaten anything since noon, and it was almost eleven.

"I'll fix you something."

"Thanks. See you in a bit."

Donovan spent a few minutes talking to the band, then said his goodbyes.

His sister leaped into his arms when she opened the door. "Hey, sis," he said, picking her up and swinging her around.

"I'm so glad to see you, Donovan." She palmed his face and examined him critically, much as their mom did each time she saw him. "You look tired. Come in." She hooked her arm in his and led him to the kitchen.

"Where's Bryce?"

"Right here," came a voice from behind them. "What's going on, Donovan? It's been a long time."

"Hey, Bryce."

"Donovan decided last minute to come to Chicago. Isn't that wonderful, honey?" Giselle asked Bryce with a twinkle in her eye. She went over to the stove. "Mom told me Terrence had a little girl. I know she's adorable. Who does she look like?"

Donovan pulled out his cell and brought up the picture of him and Nadia. "See for yourself. Her name is Nadia Elise Campbell."

Giselle took the phone, and Bryce moved closer and peered over her shoulder. "She is an absolute cutie," Giselle gushed. "You look like a natural holding her, Donovan. I can't wait to be an aunt. You're going to be such a great father."

Donovan and Bryce shared a look. Bryce grinned and mouthed, "Sorry, bro. You're on your own."

Donovan shook his head, knowing that sweet comment was just a lead-in for the inquisition that was sure to follow. His sister was a die-hard romantic and thought everyone should be happily married.

"How long are you staying, Donovan?" Bryce asked.

"I'll be here until tomorrow, then I'm going to spend a day with Mom and Dad before going back home."

"Well, I'll let you two catch up."

Donovan looked at him pleadingly.

Bryce grinned. "I have some things to do. See you in the morning." He kissed Giselle passionately.

"Yo, man, that's my sister."

"True, but she's *my* wife." Bryce winked at her and strolled out of the kitchen.

Giselle's eyes followed him until he was out of sight, a smile of contentment on her lips. Donovan remembered the same expression on Simona's face when he kissed her. Her lips had been soft and warm, and molded perfectly against his. He could kiss her for hours and never get tired of it. Thinking of Simona and her kisses sent a rush of desire straight to his groin, and he quickly claimed the nearest chair and scooted close to the table. The last thing he needed was his sister seeing his growing state.

Giselle sat a plate in front of him with a grilled chicken breast, baked potato and steamed broccoli. She poured him a glass of iced tea and herself a glass of water, then sat across from him. "So, how are things with your new lady friend?" she asked sweetly as she lifted her glass.

He groaned inwardly. "I can't even eat before you start the cross-examination, huh?"

"You're a man of many talents and multitask well. So?"

"Let's just say I'm still deciding on some things."

"Must be something serious for you to fly halfway across the country."

He glanced up from his plate. "Job, remember?"

"Whatever you say," she murmured with a smile.

"Anyway, how've you been feeling?"

"Not too bad. I had morning sickness for a few days and I get tired faster, but other than that, good."

Donovan wondered if Simona had suffered with morning sickness and whether she had gone through it alone.

"I'm going to change the sheets on the bed in the guest bedroom."

"I can do it."

She stood. "You finish your food." She placed her arm around his neck and kissed his temple. "I'm really glad to see you, Donovan."

"Same here, Gigi," he said, kissing her hand. Left alone, he scrubbed a hand down his face. What was he going to do about Simona?

Twenty-four hours later he still hadn't come up with a game plan. No, he wasn't sure he could trust her, but the only thing he had resolved in his mind was that he couldn't go another full week without holding her in his arms. Donovan spent Sunday morning and afternoon with his sister and brother-in-law, went to the concert, and then made the two-hour drive to Rockford.

He let himself into his parents' home and followed the sound of the television to the family room. "Hey, Mom, Dad."

"Donovan! Oh, my word." His mother rose swiftly from the chair and rushed over to him, examining him much like his sister had done the night before. "What are you doing here? You said you wouldn't be able to visit for a while."

Kissing her cheek and hugging her tight, he said, "I know, but I thought I'd surprise you."

"Well, you sure did that."

He moved into his father's rough hug. "You're looking good, Dad. How're you doing?"

"It's good to see you, son. I'm coming right along. How long are you staying?"

"Just till tomorrow afternoon. The group I manage had concerts in Chicago tonight and last night."

"You hungry?" his mother asked.

"No. I had dinner. But I'll take breakfast in the morning," he added with a grin.

She nodded. "Come on and sit down. What's been going on? Giselle told me you were seeing someone. Is it serious?"

Donovan shook his head and muttered, "Gigi talks too much."

His dad chuckled. "Maureen, let the boy catch his breath before you start grilling him. If he has something to tell us, he will."

Maureen Wright eyed her husband, but Elijah Wright ignored it and placed a kiss on her lips. She giggled. Donovan viewed the exchange with amusement. After nearly forty years of marriage, his father could still make his mother blush like a schoolgirl. A vision of Simona's shy smile appeared in his mind's eye. He missed her.

"You okay, Donovan?" his father asked.

"Yes, just tired." He sat and talked with his parents, catching up on the latest goings-on with relatives, his father's health and the remodeling project they were starting at the house.

His mother yawned. "It's almost midnight. I need to go to bed."

He stood and helped his mother to her feet. "Good night, Mom."

"Good night, sweetheart." She turned to her husband. "Are you coming to bed, Elijah?"

Wrapping his arms around her and kissing her, he said, "I'll be there shortly, sweetheart."

Donovan sprawled across the sofa and closed his eyes.

"Something on your mind, Donovan?"

He sat up, braced his forearms on his knees and stared at his shoes, contemplating whether to share his dilemma. Finally, he lifted his head. "Dad, I met a woman and I like her. But...I found out she has a one-year-old daughter."

"You have something against dating women with children?"

"It's not that." Though he still wasn't sure how he felt about being around a woman with another man's child. What if Donovan got attached to Yasmine and then her biological father decided to make an appearance? Who would Simona choose? "We'd been dating almost a month and she never told me. I found out when the little girl got sick and had to go to the hospital. She lied to me."

"Did she tell you she didn't have children?"

"No."

"Then she didn't lie."

"But she kept it from me, which is the same thing, in my book."

"I'm sure she planned to tell you."

"That's what she said," Donovan grumbled, still feeling a sense of betrayal.

"Son, everyone has a past, including you. If you're looking for me to validate your holding this over her head, it's not going to happen. None of us is perfect, and we all make our share of mistakes."

He opened his mouth to speak, but his father cut him off.

"There's no logic when it comes to love. This trip didn't have anything to do with your job. It had everything to do with you running away from what's going on inside. Stop listening to your head. Listen to your heart. Now I'm going to bed." He squeezed Donovan's shoulder reassuringly as he passed.

"Night, Dad." Donovan laid his head against the couch. His dad was spot on. Donovan thought the distance would ease his turmoil, but he hadn't outrun it…or his feelings. His mind said the risk was too great. But his heart wanted Simona and her little girl.

Digging out his cell, he pulled up Simona's number from his favorites list. Taking a deep breath, he tapped the screen.

"Hello."

Her soft voice came through the line and immediately warmed his heart. "Hey, Simona. How are you?"

"Okay."

"And Yasmine?"

"She's fine. Asleep for the night."

"Yeah, I guess it is pretty late. I didn't wake you, did I?"

"No."

"So, do you think we could talk?"

"I'd like that."

"I'm outside of Chicago right now, but I'll be back tomorrow night. Maybe I can come by Tuesday after you get off, if you're up for it."

"Tuesday is fine. I'll come to your office, if you don't mind."

The first thing that crossed his mind was that she had something else to hide, but he dismissed it. "All right. I'll see you then."

"Okay. Donovan, I'm really sorry and…and I've missed you," Simona added softly before disconnecting.

The sadness in her voice caused his chest to tighten. It dawned on him that he had been selfish and had never stopped to think about how hard it was, working and raising a daughter alone. Remorse filled his heart, and he promised himself that he would make it up to her.

Chapter 13

One hour to go. Simona had been doing a mental count-down since she received Donovan's call two nights ago, and now that the time had come, she wasn't sure she wanted to have the conversation. Several scenarios of what he might say cluttered her mind, making her borderline crazy. But at least she'd had the foresight to meet him at his office. That way, she could control the length of time she stayed and get out quickly if need be.

"Simona, are you applying for the job as board cleaner now?" a nurse asked as she passed, chuckling.

Simona stopped, looked up and realized that she had been erasing the same spot for the past two minutes. She jerked her hand down, replaced the eraser and shook her head. Putting Donovan out of her mind, Simona picked up the chart for her next patient and hurried off down the hallway. By the time she had a chance to breathe, her shift had ended and it was time to give the report to the incoming nursing staff.

Simona finished her report, showered and changed into a gold tank top, knee-length multicolored wrap skirt and gold wedge-heeled sandals. She slicked her lips with the MAC Oh Baby Lipglass that she wore only for special occasions, not stopping to evaluate why she was taking so much care with her appearance. At the last minute, she decided to remove the band holding her braids. She finger-combed them, surveyed her look one final time, then headed to her car.

"You look nice tonight, Simona. Going out?"

Simona froze with her hand on the car doorknob. The last person she wanted to see was Dr. Harris. She turned. "Something like that."

"I guess the rumors were true."

She lifted an eyebrow. "What rumors?"

"That you're dating someone."

"Hmm," she replied noncommittally. What she did on her off-hours was none of his business.

His jaw tightened. "I'd be lying if I said I wish you the best, so I'll just say good-night." Dr. Harris spun on his heel and stalked toward the hospital entrance.

"Good night." *And good riddance.* Simona shook her head, got into the car and drove off. Even if things didn't work out with Donovan, at least she wouldn't have to be bothered with the good doctor anymore.

The closer she got to Donovan's office, the more nervous she became. Telling him about Yasmine's birth was easy. Sharing her past relationship and her fear of the media…not so much. Although he worked primarily in the office, an integral part of his job entailed interacting with the public. If things didn't work out between them, her greatest worry was that there would be a repeat of the harassment she'd suffered previously. She couldn't, *wouldn't*, go through that again. She parked in the underground garage, took a steadying breath and got out.

Simona took the elevator to the sixth floor and walked down the silent hallway. All the doors were locked except the one at the end. Light from the outer office spilled into the dim corridor. Simona placed a hand on her belly to still the fluttering and took a cautious step inside. The secretary's desk sat empty, but she heard music coming from Donovan's office. If she left now, he would never know that she had been there, but she couldn't make her body obey. Before she lost her nerve, she crossed the floor and knocked on his open door.

He raised his head and slowly stood, his gaze taking a lingering tour up her body.

They stared at each other for a lengthy moment until she said, "Hi."

Donovan walked around his desk and came to stand in front of her. He caressed her cheek and pressed his lips against hers. "Hi. Have a seat." Taking her hand, he guided her to a small leather sofa, waiting until she was seated before he sat next to her. "You look exhausted. Long day?"

She nodded. His thumb stroking the back of her hand sent electricity up her arm. Simona gently pulled her hand away so she could gather her thoughts. "Donovan, I—"

He placed his finger against her lips. "Baby, I'm so sorry for the way I've treated you over the last two weeks. Please forgive me."

His emotionally charged words brought tears to her eyes.

"I let my past overrule my good sense and hurt you in the process."

"Your past?"

Donovan nodded. "Two years ago, my girlfriend got pregnant. I only found out when the hospital made a follow-up call after she'd miscarried. She had no intention of telling me." He paused. "I've always wondered what it would've been like to hold my little girl or boy."

Simona gasped. She could still hear the hurt in his voice and see the pain in his eyes. "I'm sorry." She couldn't imagine keeping that kind of information from the father of her child. "And you thought I was doing the same thing."

"Yes. When I walked into your house that night…" He trailed off and shook his head. "Why didn't you tell me, Simona?"

"Donovan, I had planned to tell you that night after the barbecue, in fact. I didn't say anything initially because I didn't know where this was headed. I saw no reason to bring it up if we were only going out a few times. But then I didn't want to stop seeing you, and I worried about how you'd react. Most men don't want that kind of responsibility."

Donovan got up, paced the office, then came back and sat down. "I guess I responded just like you thought. Where's Yasmine's father?"

Reaching into her purse, she took out a picture and handed it to him. He studied the smiling young couple— a man in an army uniform with his hand over the belly of a very pregnant woman. He brought the photo closer and realized the woman bore a striking resemblance to Simona, with a slightly lighter skin tone…and she was younger. A feeling of dread crawled down his spine. "Who are they?"

"That's my younger sister, Yasmine, and her fiancé, Aidan. She was twenty-two."

"Yasmine? You mean, she's…you're not…?"

"No. I'm not her biological mother. Yasmine is my niece. Her parents were killed in a car accident. Aidan died instantly. The police said they found his body wrapped around my sister, as if he was trying to protect her. My sister was seven months pregnant and died in surgery, but they were able to save her baby. The baby spent six weeks in the hospital before coming home. We thought it fitting to name Yasmine after her mother. So now you know."

Yeah, now he knew. And Donovan felt like an even bigger fool. Why hadn't he listened to her explanation in the first place? It would have saved them both some misery. "You're a remarkable woman, Simona. It had to be a big adjustment for you."

"It was. She's only been with me for two months. My grandmother was taking care of her, and I went up as often as I could to help. But Yasmine is a busy little girl, and it was getting hard for Nana to chase her around. I was fortunate enough to be able to reduce my hours, and Eve volunteered to babysit, so the transition hasn't been too bad."

"What about your parents?"

She snorted. "My parents divorced when I was sixteen and Yasmine nine. I talk to my father every now and again. He lives in Atlanta with his wife. As soon as my sister Yasmine turned eighteen, my mother said it was time to live her life. She married and divorced twice more and is currently traveling with her newest boyfriend. When baby Yasmine was born, Mom said she had already raised her children."

"Wow." He thought about his parents. Under similar circumstances, his mother would move heaven and earth to raise her grandchildren, no matter how difficult it was. They fell silent. There was still one other thing that nagged at him. He lifted Simona's hand and kissed it. "Simona, that night you said you were trying to protect Yasmine. Is someone trying to take her away from you?"

Simona stood and paced the room, wringing her hands and biting her lip.

Donovan rose to his feet and reached for her hands, his heart pounding in alarm. "Tell me what's going on, sweetheart."

"No one's trying to take her. It's nothing like that."

"Then what is it?"

"Donovan, remember I told you I like my privacy?" When he nodded, she said, "It's more than that. Before moving here, I dated a guy who was trying to make a name for himself as an actor. We were introduced by a mutual friend and hit it off pretty well. The first month or two was fine. Then every date became a publicity stunt. He promised things would change, but they didn't. I got tired of the lies. So I ended it." She stared up at him with tear-filled eyes. "He spun it to seem like he'd broken up with me and accused me of basically being a groupie. I couldn't go anywhere without a camera being shoved in my face asking all kinds of horrible questions. After they started showing up at my job, I knew it was time to leave."

His jaw tightened, and anger surged through his veins. Then it dawned on him. "And you're worried about my job."

"Yes," she whispered, swiping at an escaped tear.

Donovan gathered her in his embrace and kissed her softly. "Even if things don't work out with us, baby, I would never do that to you. I'm not that kind of man. And my mother would be on the first plane out of Chicago if she found out I disrespected a woman in any way…unless my father got to me first."

Simona laughed.

"Seriously, though, I won't let anyone hurt you or Yasmine. I don't want to give you up, Simona. I *can't*. Trust me and take a chance on us." He was glad to have her in his arms again. Although he should be focused on the conversation at hand, with her soft curves against him, he couldn't think straight. It didn't help that the moment he saw her in that sexy outfit he wanted to spread her out on his conference table. He'd expected her to show up in scrubs, but clearly she'd dressed to make a statement. He heard it…loud and clear. She had his full attention.

"I don't want to give you up, either. But he made my life a living hell, and I can't go through that again, especially not with Yasmine."

"Anyone who tries to hurt you will find out exactly what hell is like. I can promise you that." He meant every word. Thinking about what her ex put her through had Donovan seriously contemplating finding the man and beating him to a pulp. He tilted her chin to meet his eyes. "Trust me, Simona."

Simona read the sincerity in his eyes and heard the fierce protectiveness in his voice. No man had ever made her feel as safe as she did at this moment. And he had included Yasmine in his statement. "You don't have a problem dating a woman with a child?"

"Initially, I did. But actually, I'm sort of attached to her already." He shook his head. "That big grin did me in."

She laughed. "Yeah, Yasmine has that effect on people. But I'm surprised by how easily she took to you. She usually requires a warm-up period of several visits."

Donovan leaned back. "Girl, you'd better recognize. I got it like that. Yasmine knows quality when she sees it."

Her mouth gaped. "I'm not even going to comment on that. Somebody is a little arrogant."

"Arrogant, not a day in my life. Confident, yes." He shrugged. "Just sayin'."

"Wow, I'm amazed you can remain upright with that big head of yours."

He picked Simona up and swung her around, and she let out a startled yelp. "I like you, Simona Andrews. We're going to have so much fun. Starting now."

She narrowed her eyes. "What are you talking about?"

"Do you know how hard it's been for me to sit here and not touch you? From the moment you walked into my office, it was the only thing on my mind."

"What?"

"This outfit. Every time you move, that skirt reveals more and more of your gorgeous legs." His hand reached inside the opening of her skirt and caressed her thighs. "You obviously came dressed for battle, and I'm waving the white flag, baby."

His mouth came down on hers, hot and hungry, and stole her breath. His hand moved higher and around to caress her butt. He wound a fistful of her hair around his hand and tugged, gently but firmly, to expose her neck, transferring his kisses there. At the same time, Donovan glided his hand beneath her panties. She shivered and moaned as his fingers probed her slick, wet folds.

"So wet," he murmured. "Do you know how many nights I've dreamed of having you here in my office, just like this?"

"I… Oh." Surely he didn't expect her to answer. Not when his mouth and hands were on her. He slid two fingers inside her, and she cried out his name. She shuddered with need and arched against his hand, brazenly riding out his wicked rhythm. Her breath came in short gasps as the pressure built, and she screamed his name. Bolts of pleasure tore through her body.

She trembled uncontrollably and collapsed against him, her legs as weak as a newborn baby's. Donovan withdrew his fingers, picked her up in his strong arms and sat on the sofa with her cradled in his lap. She felt the hard ridge of his erection beneath her and instinctively rocked against him.

He stilled her hips. "Don't do that," he warned through gritted teeth. "As much as I've fantasized about taking you on that table over there, I want our first time to be somewhere a little more intimate so I can take my time getting to know every inch of this sexy body. But the second, third time…all bets are off."

The sensual timbre of his voice made her nipples tighten. "I can't believe I…we… What if someone came in?" His kisses had her so mindless, Simona had totally forgotten where she was.

"Everybody's gone for the day and the cleaning crew doesn't come until nine, so we're safe," Donovan said with a grin.

Immediately, she wondered why he knew that. How many other women had he brought to his office? She tried to scoot off his lap, but he held her firm.

"I know what you might be thinking, and that's not the reason. I work late a lot, sometimes until well past ten, so I know the crew. With Terrence being off, I've spent so much time here, I should have a shower and bed installed." He stood with her in his arms and lowered her to the floor. "You're the first and only woman to have christened my office. Come on, let me follow you home."

Simona adjusted her clothes and picked up her purse from the sofa. "Is there a bathroom I can use?"

He turned off the lights and locked the door. "There's one right around the corner." He pointed it out and then ducked into the men's room across the hall.

Donovan was waiting when she came out. "Speaking of Terrence," she said as they walked down the hall, "why didn't you tell me who he was beforehand?"

"Because at home, he's Terrence. Like you, he values his privacy—we both do," he added pointedly. "We've been friends since high school."

"Wait. *He's* the buddy you told me about, the one you helped start his business?"

"Yep. He really liked you. So did Janae. By the way, Janae, Audrey and Karen were concerned about you. Janae wanted your number so I gave it to Terrence. I hope you don't mind."

"No, I don't mind. I really enjoyed hanging out with them."

He made sure she was in her car before saying, "I'll be right behind you."

"Donovan, you don't have to follow me home."

"Purely selfish reasons. See you in a few."

Simona smiled and pulled out of the lot. Memories of their sensual interlude rushed back to her. "The man definitely knows his way around a woman's body." *Amen!* her inner voice agreed, with a mental high five.

Several minutes later, they arrived at her house. She got out of the car and waited for him to park. It was just past nine, and Yasmine should already be asleep. She unlocked the door and heard happy squeals. *I guess not.*

Donovan followed her inside. "Somebody's still awake, from what I can hear."

"She's probably waiting for our nightly ritual." At his confused expression, she explained. "We have to read her favorite book, sing 'Jesus Loves Me'—a nightly ritual my grandmother started—give her a backrub and kiss her stuffed animals."

He laughed. "You have to start bedtime thirty minutes earlier to get her in bed on time."

"Tell me about it." As soon as Yasmine spotted Simona, she tried to jump out of Eve's arms.

"Hold on a minute," Eve said, laughing and placing the squirming little girl on her feet.

Yasmine toddled over as fast as her legs would carry her, almost losing her balance twice. Simona picked her up and showered her with kisses. "How's my baby?" Usually, Yasmine giggled and buried her face in Simona's shoulder, but tonight someone else had captured her attention. Looking past Simona, Yasmine extended her arms to Donovan.

"I don't believe it," Simona muttered. Although she

was happy her niece had taken to Donovan, her feelings were hurt.

"Hey, angel." Donovan took Yasmine, lifted her high and placed a kiss on her belly. She squealed with delight. He kissed her cheek, and she tried to reciprocate, leaving a trail of slobber on his cheek. "Now, that's a good kiss," he said with a chuckle. She smiled and snuggled into his chest. Donovan winked at Simona. "I told you, you'd better recognize."

She rolled her eyes and folded her arms. "I can't believe you're giving him all my giggles, my kisses *and* my snuggles, Yasmine." Simona reached over and tickled her. "Little traitor." She socked Donovan playfully on the arm. "And I don't appreciate you coming in here stealing my hugs and kisses."

Eve burst out laughing. "Looks like you've been replaced, Simona. Hi, Donovan."

"Hey."

"Don't you have some studying to do?" Simona asked Eve.

Eve raised her hands in surrender. "I'm going. Donovan, nice to see you again."

"Nice seeing you, too."

"Donovan, I'm going to walk Eve to the door."

"Take your time. Yasmine and I will be just fine." He turned the baby to face Simona. "Tell your mom we're good. See you later, Eve."

"Bye, Donovan."

Hearing him call her mom stopped Simona in her tracks. It was the first time anyone had referred to her as such, and a riot of emotions bubbled to the surface. They locked eyes, and he smiled.

"Okay. I'll be right back."

"Are you all right?" Eve asked when they stood at the front door.

"Yes. It's just the first time someone has referred to me as Yasmine's mother. I'm not sure how to feel. On one hand, I'm ecstatic. On the other, I feel like I'm betraying my sister if she calls me Mom."

"You are her mother. I know you'll tell her all about your sister one day, but you will always be her mother. Now, what happened with Donovan?" she whispered. "It looks like you two have patched things up."

"For now."

"I hope it works out for you. He seems quite taken with Yasmine."

"He does, but we'll see how it goes."

"See you in the morning."

"Night."

Simona reflected on Eve's words. She could see how easy it had been for Donovan to take to Yasmine—everyone had. What concerned her was Yasmine's response to him. Simona didn't want her little girl to get too attached to him just in case he changed his mind.

But after being with Donovan tonight, and watching him interact with Yasmine, Simona didn't see how she could keep it from happening…for either of them.

Chapter 14

Donovan cradled Yasmine in his arms and rocked her as she gazed up at him contentedly. She seemed small for a one-year-old and he guessed it was because she had been a preemie. He inhaled her sweet baby scent and tried hard to remain emotionally distant, but he couldn't help himself. She had tugged on his heart that first night, but the moment she turned those big brown eyes his way and smiled at him, he was a goner. He kept up the gentle rocking, and her eyes started to close. He didn't realize he'd been singing "Jesus Loves Me" until he was somewhere around the chorus.

A smile curved his mouth when Yasmine drifted off to sleep. He placed a soft kiss on her forehead and whispered, "Sleep well, sweet baby girl."

"I didn't know you sang. You have an incredible voice," Simona said quietly behind him.

Donovan turned. "I don't know about incredible, but I can hold a tune okay."

"You also do that pretty well," she said, pointing at Yasmine.

"What? Putting her to sleep?" When she nodded, he said, "That's good to know." He planned to do the same to Simona. "Should we put her down?"

"Come on."

He followed Simona down a short hallway and stopped at the first door. She turned on a small night-light, and he made out a dresser and small toy box on one side of the room and a crib on the other. A rocking chair sat at the end of the crib. Donovan shifted Yasmine in his arms and carefully laid her in the crib. He stepped back, and Simona covered her with a light blanket, then motioned for him to follow her out.

"Will she sleep all night?" Donovan asked as they walked back down the hall and to the kitchen.

"Yes." Simona flipped a switch in the kitchen. "I'm starving. I made some chicken salad this morning. You're welcome to stay and have some if you want."

"That would be great." He wasn't ready to leave just yet.

"You have a choice of croissant, French roll or regular sliced bread."

"I'll have whatever you have. Do you need any help?"

"Nope," she answered. "It'll only take me a few minutes." Simona gestured to the kitchen table. "Have a seat."

Donovan sat at the table and watched her move around the kitchen. His eyes were glued to the skirt stretched tight across her bottom as she bent and pulled two containers and a head of lettuce from the refrigerator. His hands itched to touch her and hear her scream his name again. To distract himself, he asked, "Do you cook every night when you get off work?"

"Most nights. Then there are those times when I'll have a salad or sandwich, like tonight. Do you cook?"

He laughed. "I can cook a few things. My eggs are no

longer brown, and my steaks aren't as hard as a brick, so I consider that a success."

She turned from the counter. "You can't cook? Then how have you been eating all these years?"

"I have a housekeeper who cooks most of the time. Before that, I ate out...*a lot*, and Terrence used to take pity on me when I showed up at his house. The boy can throw down."

Simona shook her head. "That's pitiful, Donovan."

He grinned sheepishly and shrugged. "It's just me at home, so..."

She brought two plates to the table and went back for napkins and forks. "I have apple and orange juice, and water. Pick your poison."

"Orange juice." After placing the items on the table, she took a seat. "Thank you. This looks good," he said of the chicken salad sandwich on a croissant and fruit salad.

"You're welcome."

They ate in silence for a while. "What time do you have to be at work tomorrow?"

"Eleven. I get up at eight, though. Miss Yasmine will be up at eight-thirty and ready for breakfast."

He checked his watch—9:45 p.m.—plenty of time. When they finished, he insisted on washing the dishes, since she had fed him.

"You really didn't have to do the dishes," Simona said as they settled on the sofa.

Donovan drew her against him and draped his arm around her shoulder. "It was the least I could do." He traced the curve of her cheek with his finger and touched his mouth to hers, teasing the corners with tiny licks until she opened. Her tongue tangled with his, enticing and arousing him beyond any kiss he could remember. He lifted his head briefly. "You're pretty good at this."

"You think so?" She used her tongue to trace his bottom lip. "I'm just trying to keep up with you," she said seductively.

"Oh, yeah? Well, let's see how well you can keep up." Donovan used a finger to trace a path from her lips, jaw and neck to the soft, ripe rise of her breasts, and followed it with his mouth. He hooked a finger in the strap of her top and slowly dragged it down to expose a gold strapless bra. "I like this," he murmured, kissing the tops of her breasts and easing the bra down. "Mmm, but I like these even more." He circled his tongue around a taut nipple and drew it into his mouth.

"Donovan," Simona moaned.

He loved hearing his name on her lips. She grasped the back of his head and arched her body closer for more. He obliged, transferring his kisses to her other breast. Donovan repositioned their bodies until she lay flat on her back and he was stretched out over her, loving the feel of her body against his. "You are absolute perfection."

She smiled up at him while unbuttoning his shirt. "I could say the same thing about you." She ran her hands over his bare chest and abdomen. "Yeah, perfection."

His muscles contracted beneath her searing touch, drawing a low hiss from him. He reclaimed her mouth, feeding on the sweetness within. She reached between them and cupped him through his slacks. Donovan groaned. "That's dangerous territory, sweetheart. Doing that will get you in trouble."

"Is that so? You said you wanted to see if I could keep up." She moved her hand over his length and squeezed gently.

He sucked in a sharp breath. With blinding speed, he was up and had her in his arms. "Bedroom."

"Third door on the left."

Donovan strode down the hall to her bedroom and placed her on the bed. She made an alluring picture—

hair spread out over the pillow, top down around her waist, breasts still glistening and her skirt open, sensually displaying her long, toned legs. Every nerve in his body throbbed with desire.

Simona lay on her bed, her eyes riveted to the strong, muscular planes of Donovan's chest. Since that night in the hospital, she had dreamed of having her hands on him. Her gaze drifted lower to his washboard abs, trousers hanging low on a narrow waist, lean hips and muscular thighs. The expensive trousers did nothing to hide his straining erection. She jerked her gaze back to his face when he started speaking.

"If you don't want everything I have to give, tell me now. Otherwise, I'm not leaving until I put *you* to bed," he added with a wicked grin.

Her clit throbbed, and her nipples tightened. "Then put me to bed," she challenged.

A feral gleam ignited in his light brown eyes, and he chuckled low and dark. He kicked off his shoes and socks, climbed onto the bed and moved toward her like a hunter cornering his prey. "Your wish is my command."

She felt the heat of his mouth as he trailed a series of tantalizing kisses along her left ankle, her calf and behind her knee, on her outer thigh and inner thigh, then on her right side, rendering her mindless. He undid the tie on her skirt and it fell away, revealing gold boy shorts that matched her bra.

"Lovely," Donovan said as he slid them down her legs and off. "Come here, baby."

Simona sat up so he could remove her top and bra. She pushed his shirt off his shoulders, and he tossed it aside. She reached for his belt but he grabbed her hands.

"Uh-uh. Next time. I can't take your hands on me right now." He stood and shed his pants and briefs.

Her breath caught. His lean, rock-hard body was a work of art, and she wanted to explore every male inch of it. He dug his wallet out of his pants pocket and removed a condom.

With protection in place, he came back to the bed, beginning again. He gently kneaded and stroked her aching breasts and captured her mouth in a long, drugging kiss that set her aflame once more. Simona's hands glided over his strong arms, the solid wall of his chest and his back. Her hands drifted lower to his tight, ripped belly and lower still. He shifted out of her reach, and she moaned in frustration, needing him inside of her.

"Not yet."

Donovan continued to torture her with his mouth and hands—seemingly in no hurry—until she was almost delirious. She reached for him again, and he took her wrists and pinned them over her head with one hand. His other hand charted a path down the front of her body and pushed two fingers into her pulsating core. She bucked wildly and raised her hips as his fingers probed deeper. Just when she thought she couldn't take anymore, he withdrew. She whimpered.

He lightly ground his body against hers and moaned. "I love how your body feels—so soft, so smooth." Using his knee, he parted her thighs and teased the head of his erection at her entrance. "Look at me, sweetheart. I want to see your face when I enter you."

With her hands still imprisoned above her head, their eyes locked and he guided himself slowly inside until he was fully embedded. She watched the play of emotions on his face—the look of pure ecstasy. Simona understood. She felt it, too.

They both moaned. Keeping his gaze focused on her, he withdrew to the tip and slowly thrust back in, delving deeper with each rhythmic push. She wrapped her legs around his waist and locked her ankles behind his back as he kept up the sensual tempo. What he was doing to her felt so good, she didn't ever want him to stop. His strokes came faster and harder, and she cried out with pleasure. She met and matched his thrusts, their breathing growing heavier and echoing in the quiet space. Shivers of delight spread through her and she arched up higher, yearning for release.

Donovan let go of her hands, slowed his movements and groaned thickly. "I could stay inside you all night."

She moved her hips frantically and dug her fingers in his flexing butt, rocking against him, but he took his time. "Donovan," she pleaded.

He pulled her legs down and placed his thighs on either side of hers, effectively immobilizing her. "Don't move. Just feel," he whispered against her mouth, just before twining his tongue with hers at the same erotic, unhurried pace as his lower body.

The sensations were so overwhelming Simona thought she might faint. She felt every hard inch of him sliding in and out of her, the deep subtle movements burning her up from the inside out. And suddenly her body was shaking, and she came with soul-shattering intensity. Only Donovan's mouth, locked on hers, kept her from screaming loudly enough to wake the neighbors. She trembled uncontrollably for what seemed like hours, then felt him go rigid.

He tore his mouth from hers, threw his head back and let out a low, animalistic growl. His body shuddered above hers, his breathing harsh and uneven.

She closed her eyes and sucked in lungsful of air as spasms of delight rocked through her. Moments later, she opened her eyes to find him staring down at her with an expression so caring it brought tears to her eyes. He kissed her tenderly, softly and with an emotion that frightened her. In that moment, Simona knew she was in danger of losing her heart.

Donovan slid out of her and rolled over to his side, still touching and caressing her. "Where's your bathroom?"

"Right through that door," she murmured, pointing to the right while trying to keep her eyes open.

Minutes later, she felt the bed dip beneath his weight when he returned. He scooted behind her and wrapped his arm around her waist. "Sleep well."

She smiled and drifted off. Turned out he was just as good at tucking in big girls as little girls.

Donovan woke up an hour later and smiled. Simona was sleeping soundly beside him. She consistently took care of others, and he wanted tonight to be all about her. He tightened his arm around her and kissed the top of her hair. Something about this woman made him want to give her everything. And he was. As hard as he tried to hold back, he couldn't, not when she had given him her all. His mind and heart were still at odds, but the scales were starting to tilt, and he hoped he wasn't making a mistake in trusting her. He glanced over at the clock on her night-stand and sighed. For the first time in a long while, Donovan wanted to spend the night with a woman. In the past, he'd preferred to wake up in his own bed. Alone.

Moving carefully so as not to disturb Simona, he rolled over and swung his legs over the side of the bed. He retrieved his scattered clothing and dressed. Donovan quietly left the room and tiptoed into Yasmine's room to check on her. She lay on her back with her arms spread and had kicked the covers off. He covered her with the blanket and for a moment watched the rise and fall of her little chest as she slept, then he went back to Simona's room. She was sitting up with the sheet around her when he entered.

"I thought you'd left," she said softly.

Donovan observed the uncertainty in her eyes. He sat on the edge of the bed and pulled her onto his lap. "Baby, why would you think I'd leave without saying goodbye?"

Simona looked away. "Because they always do. They all promise one thing and do another."

He turned her face toward his and tucked the braids behind her ear. "I will never do that to you, and I will *always* keep my promises." He rested his cheek on top of her head and held her protectively. Her vulnerability called to him, tempted him to undress and climb back into that bed to prove to her that he was not like the men in her past. Donovan battled with himself for several minutes. "It's late, and I should be going. You have to work in the morning, and so do I."

She nodded. "I understand."

"Understand this—nothing has changed from what I told you earlier. I know men have lied to you in the past, but I meant what I said. I'll call you tomorrow."

"Okay. What time do you have to be at work?"

"Oh dark hundred," he answered with a chuckle. "Six a.m."

She scrambled off his lap, losing the sheet in the process. She snatched it back up. "It's almost one in the morning. You're going to be exhausted tomorrow."

"Maybe, but tonight was so worth it." Donovan rose to his feet and kissed her soundly. "Come lock up."

"Let me grab something to put on first."

He grinned. "Don't get dressed on my account. I like what you're wearing."

Simona rolled her eyes, but she was smiling. "I'll be out in a minute."

"What? I know you're not going to act shy, not after what we just did."

"Donovan," she whined.

"Fine, I'll go wait." He shook his head. "Get the goodies, then kick a brother out. Just cold," he muttered. Donovan stalked out with Simona's laughter following him. She joined him wearing a nightshirt that stopped midthigh and walked him to the door. She came up on tiptoe, wound her arms around his neck and kissed him with a passion that had him on the verge of carrying her back to bed.

"You sure know how to make a girl's night. Next time, it's my turn," she added with a sultry wink, running her hand over his shaft.

Blood rushed to his groin. He closed his eyes, clenched his fists and inhaled deeply. He opened his eyes to find her leaning against the wall, arms folded, with a sly grin and a challenge in her eyes. "You little tease. Good night."

She laughed softly. "Night. Drive safely."

"Always." He waited until he heard the lock click into place before going to his car. He chuckled, thinking about her bold statement. So, she thought she could make his night, huh? He looked forward to that. And he'd be ready.

Chapter 15

Despite the fact that he had gotten only three hours of sleep, Donovan arrived in the office feeling better than he had in months. He spent the first hour on the phone booking dates for Kaleidoscope's next series of concerts on the East Coast, and now sat sipping coffee while going through his emails. Promoting Monique to manage the promotions and publicity departments freed him up significantly and was one of his better moves recently. However, working things out with Simona topped his list of good decisions.

It had taken him a while to fall asleep last night because his mind had continued to race with thoughts of their love-making. And every time he thought about that kiss and her assertion that next time she would put him to sleep, he was tempted to go back to her house for that "next time."

Donovan had enjoyed every moment of being with her last night. Yes, the sex had been off the charts, but he'd also liked talking with her over sandwiches and teasing her about Yasmine giving him Simona's kisses.

Yasmine. With her wide eyes and infectious giggles, he hadn't stood a chance.

He clicked on the email from Monique. She had attached a chart she'd done on the promotional and publicity plans for each artist on the label after meeting with those department heads. *Yep, good move.* He printed it out and put it with the other weekly reports for the staff meeting.

"Is that 'Jesus Loves Me' you're humming?"

Donovan halted with the pen in his hand and glanced up to see Terrence standing in the doorway. Had he been singing? "What's up, T?"

Terrence crossed the office and took a seat across from Donovan. "That's what I came to see. And you didn't answer my question."

He shrugged. "Maybe. You have a problem with it?"

"No, but I'm curious as to why," Terrence said, stroking his goatee and studying Donovan. "Oh, and you never responded to my text Saturday."

"I was busy."

"No, you weren't. You were *running*, just like I said. Been there, done that and recognize it when I see it."

Donovan tossed down the pen and leaned back in his chair. "Fine. You were right. But for your information, I'm not running anymore. I can't. I really like Simona."

"And her daughter?"

"Yasmine isn't her daughter." He shared the circumstances of Simona's guardianship.

"So Simona's her aunt. That's pretty cool."

"She's the most giving and compassionate person I've ever met."

"I guess that means you two have made up and are together now."

"I want to make it work, but remember when I told you how she reacts when the subject of my job comes up?"

"You said she likes her privacy. Janae was the same way

when we started dating. Maybe she and Simona should talk."

"It's more than just wanting privacy. She dated an up-and-coming actor who trashed her in the media when she broke up with him, making it seem like he left her and she was nothing more than a groupie. She moved here from Oakland to get away."

"Damn. But I know you'll protect her the same way I protect Janae."

"True, but you know somewhere down the line there's bound to be something printed about us—it's the nature of this job—and I don't really know how she's going to handle it."

"You mean like this?" Terrence passed Donovan an entertainment magazine.

Donovan took the magazine and flipped to the tabbed page. "Great. This is all I need." With Simona's back to the camera and his arm around her shoulder, she was virtually unrecognizable, but he knew it was just a matter of time before a clearer photo surfaced.

"A couple of pictures of me and Janae popped up while we were dating, too, but neither of us responded so it faded pretty quickly. I'm sure that'll be the case with you two." Terrence stood. "I'd better get moving so I can be out of here by six. I'm missing my baby already."

Donovan laughed. "Nadia's got you wrapped around her pinky."

"I don't know why you're laughing. Sounds like you're not far behind."

He refused to agree with Terrence's assessment, even if it was true. "I'll be by your office later to talk to you about your tour schedule. I've gotten a few calls."

"Okay. After I clear a few things off my desk and check in with Mrs. Lewis, I'm going up to the studio. So if I'm not at my desk, that's where I'll be."

As soon as Terrence left, Donovan closed the magazine and tossed it on the corner of his desk. They had dodged a bullet this time, and he hoped their luck held. He checked the time and picked up the phone. "Vance Matthews," he said, greeting the man on the other end of the phone.

"Donovan Wright," came the booming reply. "Hey, man. I haven't talked to you since you were out at the house a few months back. How ya been?"

He laughed. They had been greeting each other this way since high school. "Good. How's Belinda?"

"She's married to me. How do you think she's doing?"

"That's why I'm asking. I don't know how she's put up with you all these years."

"At least I've got a woman. Hell, even Terrence is married."

"Whatever, man. Anyway, I need a few passes to Disneyland. Belinda said she'd get me some whenever I needed them."

"Ah, the real reason for this early morning call. Hold on. Hey, Lindy, Donovan's on the phone," Donovan heard him yell. "He wants those Mickey passes you promised."

A moment later a soft voice came through the line. "Hi, Donovan. How many do you need?" Belinda worked at the Walt Disney Studios.

"Hey, Belinda. I'm not sure. There's a special lady I'd like to take who's never been."

"You're in luck. My brother was supposed to visit but had to cancel, so I have nine or ten park hopper tickets."

"Park what?"

"Park hopper. You can go to both Disneyland and California Adventures."

He hadn't been to Disneyland in a long time and had forgotten about the second park. "That would be great."

"You're welcome to take them all. Give them away or

take her again. We'll be here after seven tonight, if you want to come by."

"Thanks, Belinda. You're the best. I'll be over after I leave work tonight." Donovan ended the call and smiled. Now it was time to show Simona that he was a man who kept his promises.

Simona waved at the security guard who had walked her to her car and drove out of the hospital lot. Between her busy day and late night, she was beyond tired, but as Donovan had said, it had been *so* worth it. She'd never doubted his bedroom skills but hadn't expected the tenderness, which made it harder to keep from falling for him. She yawned. *I hope Yasmine isn't in a playing mood tonight.* That morning, the little munchkin had been all smiles and babbling nonstop.

As soon as she entered her house, her cell rang. Simona prayed it wasn't the hospital calling her back for an additional shift. Seeing Donovan's name on the display made her smile.

"Hi, Donovan."

"Hey, baby. I know you're just getting off work, so I won't hold you long."

"It's fine. Actually, I'm just walking in the house."

"If you're not busy on Saturday, I'd like to take you and Yasmine to Disneyland. As a matter of fact, I have enough passes for Eve and her sisters' families, if they want to go, too."

"Wow. Are you serious?"

"I promised you I'd take you, didn't I? And I wanted to make up for being so bullheaded and not listening to your explanation."

Her heart softened a little more. He told her he kept his promises, and he was proving it. "Yes, you did, and it wasn't all your fault."

"Can you find out if the others want to go and let me know?"

"I'll ask and call you tomorrow. Thank you, Donovan."

"Anytime. Kiss Yasmine for me, and get some rest. I know you need it after your day."

"I will. Good night." She stood in the middle of the living room and held the phone against her chest. *I'm falling in love with this man.*

"Simona, are you okay?"

"I'm fine, Eve. I was talking to Donovan." She bent to pick up her niece, who was banging on Simona's leg. "Hi, sweetie. How was your day?" Simona sat on a chair in the dining room with Yasmine in her lap while Eve packed up her books. "Donovan has Disneyland tickets and wants to invite you, your sisters and their families on Saturday."

"That's nice of him. Those tickets aren't cheap. I haven't been there in years, and it might be a nice relaxer after I get done with this final on Thursday. I'm never taking a summer session again. My brain is fried."

Simona laughed. "I know what you mean. I thought I was going to die when I did that master's in nursing."

"I'm going to try to put in about three more hours of studying, and I'll call my sisters tonight to ask them. Girl, Donovan is a keeper. See you tomorrow."

Later, while lying in bed, Eve's words rushed back to Simona: *Donovan is a keeper.* She wanted to believe he was a keeper, and so far, he had not broken any of his promises, but every relationship started that way. Would he still keep them next week, or a month from now? *One day at a time,* she told herself.

She was admittedly excited about her first trip to Disneyland, and by Saturday was bouncing off the walls like a kid on Christmas morning. She finished packing Yasmine's bag with milk, food, snacks, diapers, a change of clothes and everything else she thought she might need.

Even Yasmine seemed to sense Simona's enthusiasm because she was more animated than usual. Eve and her sisters' families had agreed to join them, and everyone would meet at Simona's house at nine. Due to the children's young ages, they all felt it better to go early. Donovan arrived at a quarter to nine.

"Morning. How are my girls?" he asked, wrapping an arm around her waist and kissing Simona with a hunger that left her lightheaded.

"Mmm, morning. We're good." Yasmine kicked her legs excitedly, squirmed in Simona's arms and grabbed Donovan's shirt. "Hold on, little girl. It's a good thing I got my kisses," Simona teased, and passed her to Donovan.

"Hey, angel." Donovan placed noisy kisses all over her face, and Yasmine squealed with delight. He turned to Simona. "Do you need me to help you pack anything for her?"

"Nope. It's all done. We just need to transfer the car seat." She went to retrieve her car keys from the hook in the kitchen.

"Okay. I'll do it." He eased the keys from her hand.

"You sure? Those things aren't easy to put in."

"Yeah. I'll have to learn sooner or later, preferably sooner." He handed Yasmine back and strolled out the door.

Simona stood stunned by his words. Did she dare hope that he planned to stay around? Smiling, she placed Yasmine on her feet. "All right, little one, let's go to Disneyland."

Twenty minutes later, they were on the road. Eve rode with Simona and Donovan, while her siblings and their families followed in an SUV large enough for both couples and their children. When they arrived at the large theme park, Eve's brother-in-law paid the parking for both cars. Simona chuckled at the strollers and bags that had to be unloaded. With all the stuff they had, someone would think they planned to be at the park for a week.

"You didn't have to pay for the parking," Donovan told Eve's brother-in-law as they walked toward the entrance.

"Man, it was the least I could do, since you wouldn't take any money for the tickets."

Simona found out that Donovan had secured tickets for both parks. He let her choose the first stop, and she opted for Disneyland.

Donovan took her hand as soon as they passed the gates. "Simona, whatever you want to do and see, or wherever you want to go, let me know. This day is for you, and I want it to be special."

Just like that, another layer dropped off her heart. "Thank you, Donovan."

Simona had a ball. They took the children to It's a Small World and Goofy's Playhouse, rode the Disney Railroad and Jungle Cruise. Yasmine spent more time on Donovan's shoulders than in her stroller. She wanted to be in his arms every minute. But Simona couldn't blame her because it was the same place she wanted to be. Donovan convinced Simona to ride Space Mountain, the Indiana Jones Adventure and The *Twilight Zone* Tower of Terror. It took at least an hour for her stomach to settle after all those drops.

Later, the group had lunch in one of the character dining restaurants. The kids, especially Eve's five-year-old niece, got a kick out of seeing and taking pictures with the Disney characters. Simona ate and watched as Donovan patiently fed Yasmine. The little girl was far more interested in his mashed potatoes and ate more off his plate than her own food.

"Do you want me to take her so you can eat?" Simona asked.

"No. She's fine. I can't believe she eats this much. Whoa,

angel." Donovan grabbed hold of his plate just before Yasmine pulled it off the table.

Simona laughed. "Oh, and those little hands are fast."

"Tell me about it. So, are you enjoying yourself?"

"I'm having a great time. I feel like a kid again. But I'm never going near the Tower of Terror again." She rolled her eyes. "You said it wasn't that bad."

He laughed. "It wasn't." He leaned closer and nuzzled her neck. "Come on, admit it, you had fun."

She giggled. "I'm not admitting anything."

"You don't have to. I know you loved it."

"Whatever, Donovan Wright. Eat your food."

He winked and unleashed that captivating smile on her, then kissed the top of Yasmine's head and continued to eat.

Simona's heart leaped. She didn't think she would ever get used to that smile.

"Girl, I see what you meant," Eve said, sotto voce. "That smile, those eyes and, *mercy*, that dimple! A lethal combination guaranteed to make a woman drop her panties every time. Now I know why that grin has been a permanent fixture on your face lately."

She felt her face grow warm. He could make her drop her panties and more, just from the lightest touch. A vision of him running his hands all over her body filled her mind.

"Stop that," Eve whispered.

Simona whipped her head around. "What?"

Grinning, she said, "Those must have been some thoughts. Your whole expression changed."

"I don't know what you're talking about," Simona mumbled, pushing the food around her plate. She met her friend's amused face and couldn't hide her smile.

As they left the restaurant, Donovan said, "There's another ride I want to take you on. I promise you'll like this one. No big drops."

She wagged a finger his way. "Okay, but I'm warning you…"

Eve volunteered to keep an eye on Yasmine.

Donovan led her inside a vintage airplane hangar with a sign that read Soarin' Over California, then to a briefing room and finally into a large theater. After they were strapped in, the lights went off and the huge screen came to life. Simona sat mesmerized by the foggy skies clearing to reveal the Golden Gate Bridge. She felt as if she were flying over the city. She couldn't contain her delight when she smelled oranges as they passed over the groves, or the pine scent and cold in snowy Lake Tahoe. Simona instinctively covered her face as a golf ball flew toward her, but relaxed viewing the lights of downtown Los Angeles's nightlife. The ride came to an end, and they followed the crowd to the exit.

"Oh, my God! That was *fantastic*!" she squealed as soon as they were outside, launching herself into his arms. "This has been one of the best days ever." She kissed him deeply, trying to convey her feelings. "Thank you, thank you *so* much for bringing me here. I lo—" She clamped her jaws shut and backed out of his arms.

Donovan pulled her back into his arms. "What were you going to say?"

"Just that I loved the ride," she answered quickly.

He eyed her a lengthy minute before saying, "I'm glad."

"We'd better head over to California Adventures, if we're going. The kids will be worn out soon." She took his hand and guided him back to where the others waited, chastising herself for almost blurting out those words. *What were you thinking, Simona?* She would have liked to attribute the surge of emotions to being caught up in the spectacular day, but she knew it was a lie. She was falling in love with him, plain and simple.

For the rest of the afternoon and all the way home, every

time their eyes met, Donovan stared at her curiously. She tried to avoid direct eye contact, but he made it difficult. He helped unload the car and placed the sleeping Yasmine in her crib. The day had worn her out, and she didn't stir while Simona changed her diaper and put on her pajamas.

She stalled going back into the living room where Donovan waited, but after several minutes she walked back down the hallway. She found him stretched out on the sofa with his eyes closed.

"Come here, sweetheart." He held his hand out to her.

She placed the baby monitor on the table, then spooned her body next to him.

"Tired?"

"Yeah, but in a good way. I wanted to see more."

Donovan chuckled. "There's no way to see it all in one day. We'll go back another time and spend a day at each park."

"I'd like that." They'd stayed only a couple of hours at California Adventures because the kids were getting cranky. Simona really wanted to ride Soarin' Over California again, but had pushed the desire away and, instead, made sure they squeezed in as many kiddie rides as possible in that short period.

They lay quietly for a long while, then Donovan said, "My next week is going to be pretty hectic, and I'll have to pull some weekend hours. Maybe the weekend after, we can go on a picnic or to the park for a while."

"Actually, I'm going to Oakland that weekend. Nana misses Yasmine, and I promised to bring her up there."

He groaned. "I can't go two weekends without spending time with you, baby." He rolled onto his back and pulled her on top of him. "I need to see you." He removed the band from her hair, and the braids cascaded around her face. He fisted his hands in her hair and crushed his mouth against hers.

Intense desire shot through her body like a crack of lightning. He released her hair, and then his hands were on her body. She felt him everywhere. Her nipples hardened against his chest, and a deep ache settled between her thighs. He broke off the kiss abruptly and palmed her face, his smoldering light-brown gaze searing her. He'd once said her eyes told him everything he needed to know, so Simona quickly turned away and laid her head on his shoulder, afraid he would read her emotions.

"Simona, baby. Look at me."

She slowly lifted her head.

"Tell me—"

"Mamamama…anana…" His words were cut off by the sound of babbling coming from the monitor.

She scooted off his body and rushed out of the room, grateful for the interruption. Donovan eventually left so she could settle Yasmine, but the look he gave her before walking out the door said the conversation was far from over.

Although he hadn't given her a reason not to believe in him, she wasn't ready to share what lay in her heart: that she had fallen in love with him.

Chapter 16

Donovan smiled at the text from Simona on Monday morning: Ugh! Disneyland withdrawals.

He typed back: It's only been two days, but anytime you want to go again... He had gone to amusement parks several times as a teen and twice as an adult, and always enjoyed himself. However, none of those visits compared to the amazing time he'd had on Saturday. In the past, he'd always thought people who brought very young children to those parks had to be crazy, but Yasmine's happy face—as well as those of the other three children—had changed his perspective. He relished the sounds of their delightful chatter. It hadn't even bothered him when Yasmine seized a fistful of his mashed potatoes and shoved them into her mouth, or when she wiped that same hand on his shirt.

As priceless as those memories were, nothing topped Simona's reaction to the Soarin' Over California ride. His heart swelled, and the magnitude of that moment would forever be imprinted on his brain—it was the moment he knew he had fallen in love with her. When she threw her arms around him and kissed him, he'd have sworn she was about to tell him she loved him. He hadn't been able to coax the words from her then or later that night. Donovan didn't realize how much he wanted to hear her say it. Maybe he should have said it first, but he wasn't ready to put his heart on the line.

"Hey, D. You have a minute?"

Donovan tossed the phone on his desk. "What are you still doing here? I thought you left an hour ago."

Terrence entered and dropped a notepad on Donovan's desk.

"What's this?"

"Lyrics I'm working on for my next song. I want you to take a look."

He picked up the pad and scanned the words. "Ballad?" When Terrence nodded, Donovan asked, "What's the title?"

"Without Your Love."

Taking inspiration from his newly discovered feelings, Donovan picked up his pen, added a few lines, tweaked three others and handed the pad back.

Terrence glanced down at the paper, then back to Donovan, and lifted an eyebrow. "Something you want to tell me?"

"No."

"Hmm. I haven't been able to get you to pick up that pen and write one word in eight years, and you perfect my song in, like, two minutes? Must be love."

Donovan merely shrugged.

"Ah, so I'm right. So, are you in denial?"

"No. Unlike some other people, I don't have a problem owning up to my feelings. I just think she's still a little uneasy because of her ex, so I have my work cut out for me."

"Stepping up your game, I see."

"My game is fine," Donovan retorted.

Terrence laughed. "If you say so. Now that the song is

finished, I'm going home." He turned back when he got to the door. "You should really consider donning your songwriter's hat again."

"Nah, I'm good."

"Why not? The three songs we co-wrote and the one you wrote were among my biggest hits."

"I know. But my name better not be anywhere near those liner notes when you're done with this project."

Terrence shook his head. "Okay. You're the only person I know who doesn't want to take credit for his work. Later."

"Later." Donovan didn't plan to trust Terrence this time—he'd said the same thing nine years ago, and Donovan ended up with credits on at least four songs. He made a mental note to follow up with the art department before that CD hit the shelves.

Donovan and Simona had only had a few brief conversations, due to his schedule and her working extended shifts, and by the weekend Donovan missed Simona more than he'd imagined. He desperately wanted to see her, but had to meet with Brad—who had been out of the office all week—to hammer out the details of Kaleidoscope's next tour contract. He wasn't too keen on the promoter's proposed date changes, which didn't leave much time for the group to recover between the concerts and attend the additional local promotions, interviews and autograph signings. The back-and-forth had put them behind schedule, and Donovan wanted to lock in the dates as soon as possible. Though the first date was six months away, he wanted the publicity department to get started.

He and Brad spent three hours reworking the contract with the hopes that the changes would be acceptable to the promoter. Donovan's biggest concern was building in a small cushion of time between tour stops.

Brad left at five-thirty and Donovan toyed with waiting until Monday to add the notations to the contract, but remembered he and Terrence had three consecutive meetings with prospective clients.

Donovan stood, stretched and massaged his neck in an attempt to loosen the muscles. He moved back to his desk to catch his ringing cell. Seeing Simona's name on the display put a smile on his face.

"Hey, baby."

"Hi, Donovan. Did I catch you at a bad time?"

"No. Just taking a quick break before I get back to work."

"I thought you were only going to be there a short time."

He blew out a long breath. "So did I. But we had to address some problems with one of the contracts. I should make it out of here by seven, or seven-thirty at the latest. I know you had to work some long hours this week, too. What you do is far more tiring. How are you doing?"

"I took a nap with Yasmine earlier, so I'm okay. I know you have to get back to work. I just wanted to hear your voice and check on you."

He wanted to sit on the phone and listen to her sweet voice all night, but knew he should hang up. "And hearing your sexy voice made my night. I'm going to try to get out of here at a decent hour. If you're not busy tomorrow, I'll come by."

"That's fine. I'll see you tomorrow if you're not too tired."

"Kiss Yasmine for me."

"I will."

The fact that Simona had taken time to check on him made Donovan love her more. No matter what it took, he needed to keep her in his life.

Simona hung up and placed the cordless on the base. She missed hearing Donovan's voice, seeing his smile, laughing with him. She just missed *him*. And she wanted to see him…today. An idea popped into her mind, and she smiled. Before she could lose her nerve, she snatched up the phone again and called Eve.

"Hey, Eve. Could you watch Yasmine for a couple of hours?" When her friend agreed, she explained her plan. After disconnecting, she rushed to her room to get ready.

Turning first one way then the other in the mirror, she nodded, pleased with her look. "Donovan, I hope you like surprises," she mumbled.

Thirty minutes later, Simona made her way down the hallway leading to the administrative offices of RC Productions like a woman on a mission. Several times during the drive she almost changed her mind. She had never done something so bold in all her life, and the closer she came to Donovan's office, the colder her feet got. She passed the restroom, and another crazy idea crossed her mind.

"Don't even think about it, Simona," she told herself. But she had come this far, so why not go for broke?

Like last time, she heard the music as soon as she rounded the corner. She crossed the outer office, stood in the doorway of Donovan's office and just observed him. His head was down, and his hand moved quickly across the paper. He was seated so she could see only the black T-shirt. After staring at him a good two or three minutes, she decided to make her presence known.

"Looks like you could use a break."

His head came up sharply, and his mouth fell open. "Simona?"

Simona chuckled inwardly at the stunned expression on his face. She trembled as his heated gaze charted a path down her body, leaving a blaze in its wake, and knew she had made the right decision in coming. "You've been working really hard this week, and I'm sure you haven't gotten much sleep. I think you need a nap."

"Huh? Wait, what?"

He seemed confused for a moment, then she saw the moment her message clicked in his mind. Something wicked and dark flashed in his eyes, and Donovan was up in the blink of an eye and around the desk. He hauled her into his arms, and his mouth came down on hers...*hard*. His tongue swirled around hers in a kiss so devastatingly erotic it left her gasping for breath and pulsing everywhere.

She reached up and caressed his cheek. "I came to fulfill my promise," she whispered against his lips before kissing him again. She captured his tongue and sucked gently, causing a low growl to erupt from his throat.

Donovan broke off the kiss and lifted his head. He held Simona away from him and feasted his eyes on the vision of loveliness standing before him. When he'd looked up to find her standing in the doorway in that sexy dress, he almost came right then and there. The fire-red strapless dress stopped midthigh and hugged every delectable curve as if it had been created specifically for her. And those red stilettos...he sucked in a deep breath to gain a measure of control.

"Are you ready, baby?"

"I'm ready for anything you have to give. I hope you brought your A-game."

"Oh, I did, so let's see who wins," she said with a sultry purr, tossing her braids over one shoulder.

Donovan went to lock both the outer and inner office doors and came back to find her standing in the same spot. She backed him toward the loveseat, pushed him down and straddled his lap. She looped her arms around his neck, leaned in and nibbled on his bottom lip, teasing and tormenting him. He gripped her thighs, and she pushed his hands away.

"Don't touch me. Not yet."

He groaned. "I need to touch you, Simona."

She smiled and shook her head. "No." Simona reached for the hem of his shirt and pulled it up and over his head. "I love touching you, Donovan," she murmured, lightly running her hands over his face, neck, shoulders and chest.

Her warm tongue skated across his chest and along his jaw, exciting him and making his erection throb. He arched up and tried to grind his body against hers, but she moved just out of his reach. She continued to torture him with her hands and tongue until he thought he would explode.

His head fell back against the loveseat. "Baby," he panted. "I can't take this. I gotta—" He jerked upright and gasped sharply when she reached inside his shorts and closed her hand around his shaft. She slowly slid her hand up and down his length, and all he could do was grit his teeth to keep from shouting. He couldn't even begin to explain the passion she aroused in him. Never in all his life had anyone made him feel this way. No other woman. On the verge of coming, he grasped her hand and brought it to his lips. "No more."

She smiled, hooked her fingers in the waistband of his shorts and pulled them down and off. "Very impressive." She stood and tossed them to the side.

"Why am I the only one naked?" he asked, scooting forward and caressing her legs. His hands glided along her thighs, under her dress and up to cup her bottom. He froze. "Simona Andrews, where are your panties?" Donovan asked with surprise.

She chuckled. "Are you complaining?"

"Hell, no. But—"

"Good." She unzipped the dress and let it drop to the floor, leaving her wearing nothing but those heels.

For the second time that night, Donovan's jaw came unhinged. She straddled his lap, sensuously grinding her body against his. He sank his hands into her hair and fused their mouths together. Their low moans echoed throughout the office. His hands feathered over her back and down her hips to bring her closer. He lifted her hips and prepared to enter her. Suddenly, sanity returned. He didn't have any protection. What if he pulled out in time? Who was he kidding? But even if she got pregnant...

Whoa! What am I saying? He must be out of his mind to even contemplate tempting fate. Kissing the shell of her ear, he said, "We might have to get creative. As bad as I want to make love to you, I can't. I don't have any protection."

"But I do," Simona said breathlessly, rising to retrieve it from her purse sitting on his desk.

Hallelujah! She tore open the package and knelt in front of him. Donovan reached for it, but she shook her head, eyes glittering with mischief. She rolled it over his erection excruciatingly slow, driving him to the brink of insanity. Simona climbed onto his lap, her breasts at the perfect height. He cupped one in each hand and gently massaged the sweetly curved mounds, then lowered his head and captured a swollen nipple between his lips, tugging gently. He lifted her hips and guided her down on him with one smooth thrust.

"Yessss!"

She placed her hands on his shoulders, lifted her body until only the head of his shaft remained, then lowered herself gradually back down, gyrating in deliberate, insistent circles, repeating the cycle several times. Donovan threw his head back and groaned loudly. She kept up the maddening pace until he couldn't take it anymore. He tightened his grip on her hips and drove up into her, pulling her down to meet his deep, forceful thrusts.

"Donovan, baby," Simona gasped. She leaned back, braced one hand on his thigh and rode him hard and fast.

He swore hoarsely and grew even harder, his breathing harsh and uneven. She was trying to kill him. Intense heat radiated through his body, and he changed the tempo to prolong their pleasure. Without missing a beat, he rose from the sofa and placed her on the conference table, ready to act out his fantasy.

"Do you know how amazing you are?" He swiped his tongue across her nipple, and she cried out.

She returned the gesture. "Do you know how amazing *you* are?"

He smiled and started moving again. Soon his thrusts came faster, and she lifted her hips to match his fluid movements. Donovan draped her legs over his shoulders, planted his feet and pumped in and out of her, groaning from the extreme pleasure flowing through his body.

"More, Donovan. Please, don't stop," she chanted.

"Don't worry, sweetheart."

"Donovan!" Her walls clenched him tight as she convulsed all around him. Simona let out a high-pitched scream, and her back came up off the table.

Donovan withdrew, released her legs, turned her around and surged back inside her. Simona screamed again. He nearly lost control at the sight of her bent over his table, hair all wild, velvety brown skin glistening and those red shoes. He leaned down and rained kisses along her spine, then closed his eyes and started thrusting in long, deep strokes, delving deeper with each rhythmic push.

She did that hip swirl thing again, and he lost it. He stroked her harder and faster, and he felt her walls closing in on him as she came again. A rush of pleasure shot through his body and he exploded inside her, yelling her name. His body trembled violently, and his head fell forward limply as he took deep, shuddering breaths to try to force oxygen into his lungs.

When he could move, Donovan lifted Simona in his arms, carried her to the sofa and sat with her in his lap.

"You all right, baby?" he asked.

"Mmm," she answered.

Donovan chuckled.

"What's so funny?"

"You win. Good night," he said tiredly. He felt her smile against his chest. As sleep claimed him, he murmured, "I love you, Simona."

Simona's head came up sharply. "What did you say?" *Did he just say he loves me?* "Donovan?" No answer. His chest rose and fell in measured rhythm. He had fallen asleep. She studied him as he slept, and noticed the tired lines etched in his handsome face. A smile curved her lips. She reached up and lightly traced his mouth and kissed him. "I love you, too." Snuggling against his chest, she closed her eyes and drifted off.

Sometime later, she felt a gentle shake on her shoulder. Groaning, she mumbled, "What time is it?"

"Almost nine. But don't worry, the cleaning crew doesn't come in tonight," Donovan added.

Good thing because there was no way she could be up and dressed in the next few minutes. Her body was stiff from the intense workout they'd had. She smiled contentedly.

"What are you smiling about?"

She sat up. "How did you know I was smiling?"

"I could feel it."

"I was just thinking about earlier."

"Woman, I'm going to have to ban you from my office," he said, shaking his head. "I don't know how I'm ever going to get any work done because after tonight, every time I step foot in here, I'll be thinking about you and these shoes." He lifted her foot.

"Actually, this is the first time I've worn the dress and

the shoes. A friend of mine back home talked me into buying them, but I never got up the nerve to wear them."

"Until tonight."

"Until tonight," she echoed. Simona debated whether to bring up what he had said before he fell asleep. What if he hadn't really meant to say it? She wanted to ask the question badly, but held back because she wasn't ready to confess her own feelings or get her hopes up for something that might not last.

"Now, as much as I would love to lie here all night with you, this little couch isn't made for extended comfort."

She laughed. "I need to go home anyway. Yasmine is probably still up looking for me."

"You're right, I'm sure. So let's get moving." He quickly dressed, then excused himself to go to the bathroom.

As she dressed, she thought about Donovan's words. The way he treated her and Yasmine was nothing short of amazing. And he did confess to loving her. Could she really let go? Hope sprang in her chest. Maybe…

She went to retrieve her purse from his desk, and the cover of an entertainment magazine caught her eye. Sheila Martin was on the cover. Simona turned to the page, and her heart nearly stopped. Someone had taken a photograph of her and Donovan at the backstage party. The picture was of another fan in attendance with Simona and Donovan in the background.

Although her back was to the camera and the shot not clear, it was all she needed to confirm that this relationship couldn't work. It would be a matter of time before she was in the headlines again. She replaced the magazine just before he returned. She had to get out of here.

"Simona, are you okay?"

"I'm fine," she answered quickly. "It's late. I'd better get going." She reached up and kissed him on the cheek. "I'll see you later."

"Hold on a minute, baby. Let me walk you out."

"No." At his confused stare, she said, "You don't need to do that. I'm parked right next to the elevator. Go ahead and finish up your work so you're not here all night."

He folded his arms across his chest and continued to scrutinize her. "What's going on? You seem a little... I don't know."

"Nothing's going on. Just a little tired." Donovan's expression said he didn't believe her for a minute, but she was thankful he didn't question her further. "Good night."

Donovan grabbed her by the hand and said, "Let's go."

Donovan sat in his office after Simona left, puzzled by the change in her demeanor. One minute she was all smiles, and the next it seemed as if she had regrets.

He called her when he got home to make sure she was all right, and she all but rushed him off the phone. For some reason she was pulling away, and he wanted to know why. Something had happened between the time he had gone to the bathroom and the time he'd returned, and he intended to find out what.

The first part of his week kept him so busy, including an overnight trip, that he and Simona talked for only a few minutes on Tuesday. Two days later, he found himself on her doorstep after work.

"Donovan. Hey. What are you doing here?" Simona asked, clearly surprised.

"I just came to check on you. Can I come in?"

She hesitated for a split second then stepped back. He followed her to the living room.

"Yasmine in bed already?"

"Yes."

Usually, she sat next to him on the sofa, but tonight she chose one of the chairs. "Simona, did I do or say something wrong?"

"No. Why?"

"You've been acting strange."

"I'm fine. Things at work have been a little more stressful lately, that's all."

"Is there anything I can do?"

She shook her head. "I'm sure it'll calm down soon."

He nodded. She wasn't telling him the truth. In the back of his mind, he wondered if she was hiding something else. Donovan stood and pulled Simona to her feet. He wrapped an arm around her waist and tilted her chin. "You'd tell me if there was a problem, wouldn't you?"

"There's no problem, Donovan. You don't need to worry." She gave him a quick kiss. "I have to go in early tomorrow, so…"

"So do I. How about I take you to the airport on Saturday?"

"Oh, no. That's okay. Eve already said she'd take me. You don't have to come all the way over here."

His brow lifted in suspicion. "It's no trouble."

"I know. I'll just see you when I get back."

Their eyes held for a long moment, then he nodded. Lowering his head, he slanted his mouth over hers in a gentle, reassuring kiss. "Call me when you get there."

"Okay."

He kissed her once more and slipped out the door. Simona kept insisting there was nothing wrong, but she'd refused his offer to take her to the airport and was quiet… almost distant.

Later, after showering, he pulled out his laptop and searched flights to Oakland. She mentioned leaving late morning, so he booked an earlier flight.

He was going after her.

Chapter 17

Simona arrived in Oakland after noon the following Saturday. She deplaned and stopped short, shocked to see Donovan waiting. A wave of panic bubbled up inside her. What was he doing here? And how long had he been waiting? She had spent the past week trying to distance herself from him, and now he had followed her. Of course, Yasmine was happy to see him and nearly jumped out of Simona's arms trying to get to him.

Donovan placed a soft kiss on Simona's lips, took Yasmine and kissed her forehead. "I know something is wrong. Whatever it is, we can work it out." Donovan collected Simona's suitcase, and Yasmine's stroller and car seat from the baggage carousel. "I need to pick up my car from the rental center."

"My grandmother is picking me up. I told her I'd call when I got here," she told him, trying to buy a little more time.

"There's no need for her drive here when I'm already here. So you can call her and tell her you have a ride."

She started to argue, but the look on his face left no room for negotiation. She called her grandmother and gave her a hasty explanation. Simona walked next to Donovan while pushing the stroller. She glanced down at Yasmine banging on the toy affixed to the front of it. She had done surprisingly well, considering it was her first flight.

Once they were secured in the Cadillac SRX crossover, he plugged her grandmother's address into the GPS and pulled out of the lot. As they drove, Simona couldn't help but remember her last months of living in Oakland, which added to her list of worries. She closed her eyes to shut out the unwanted memories. As if sensing her unease, Donovan rested his hand on top of hers and gave it a gentle squeeze.

"You okay?"

"Yeah." Changing the subject, she said, "I should probably warn you that my grandmother can be a little blunt and overprotective, especially where men are concerned."

"I'm sure we'll be fine."

"I don't know."

Donovan cut her a look. "Please, your grandmother's going to love me."

Despite the tension between them, he always knew how to make her smile. Simona rolled her eyes. "Here we go again with the big head."

"What? You don't think I'm a loveable guy?"

"No comment," she said, trying to hide her smile.

"Uh-huh, that's what I thought. Don't you think I'm loveable, Yasmine?" he said, glancing in the rearview mirror.

As if she recognized that someone was talking to her, Yasmine started babbling.

Donovan laughed. "Tell her, baby girl."

Simona whipped around in her seat and was met with

a big grin. She turned back and punched Donovan in the shoulder.

He laughed harder.

She folded her arms, stared out the window and bit her lip to keep from laughing, too. When they pulled up in front of her grandmother's house, Frances Walker was out of the house and striding down the sidewalk with a speed that belied her age. Simona jumped out of the car and met her halfway. Nana engulfed Simona in a tight hug, rocking her side to side.

"I'm so glad to see you, baby. I've missed you so much," she said emotionally.

"I missed you, too, Nana."

She released Simona and palmed her face. "Let me look at you. You look good." She brought Simona in for another crushing hug. "Where's my great-grandbaby?"

By this time, Donovan had taken Yasmine out of her seat and was coming toward them.

"Ooh, you were right. He's really good-looking. Nice body, too," Nana whispered with a giggle.

Great. One more female who can't resist this man. "Nana, this is Donovan Wright. Donovan, this is my grandmother, Frances Walker."

"It's a pleasure to finally meet you, Mrs. Walker. Simona has told me nothing but good things about you."

She waved him off. "Oh, you can call me Nana."

Donovan unleashed his full smile, dimple and all. "Nana it is." He bent and kissed her cheek.

Simona's jaw dropped when Nana blushed like a schoolgirl. Donovan winked at her, and she scowled at him.

"You all come on in." Nana reached for Yasmine, and the little girl clung to Donovan.

"Well, I'll be," Nana said.

"Welcome to my world," Simona muttered.

Donovan handed Yasmine to Nana. "Go talk to Nana. I have to get the bags, okay?"

"Hey, sweet pea. Ooh-wee, Nana's gonna spoil you rotten over the next two days," she said as she carried Yasmine into the house.

Simona shook her head and followed Donovan to the car.

"I like Nana," Donovan said as Simona approached.

"Apparently the feeling is mutual," she groused.

"Don't hate. I told you…I got it like that." He placed a quick kiss on her lips.

"Shut up and come on."

He roared with laughter.

Inside, she directed him to the bedroom she always used when she stayed over and he set down her luggage. "Um, Nana said you should stay here at the house."

"I planned to stay at a hotel."

"She kind of insisted. I think she wants to check you out. Let me show you to your room." Simona walked farther down the hall to a room that held another queen-size bed.

"I'll get my bag in a few minutes." He glanced around. "This is nice. Who are those people in the pictures?"

She looked up and pointed. "These two are my grandfather, and this one is my uncle. My grandfather died nine years ago, and my uncle lives in Boston. Let's go see what Nana's giving Yasmine that she shouldn't have."

Simona spent the afternoon catching up with Nana and observing how she interacted with Donovan. So far, she seemed to like him. Every now and then Simona would catch him scrutinizing her. She knew she would have to tell him about seeing the picture.

"Don't you two want to go out or something?" Nana asked later.

"Nana, I don't want to leave you here with Yasmine.

She can be a handful." And she didn't want to be alone with Donovan.

"And so were you at this age. We'll be just fine. She's already had dinner, so we're just going to entertain ourselves until bedtime." She divided a speculative look between Simona and Donovan. "Besides, you should show Donovan around."

"Are you sure, Nana?" She chanced a glance in his direction and found him smiling. *Of course.*

"Sure I am. Donovan, don't you want to do some sightseeing? Y'all can go over to Jack London Square or something."

The mention of Jack London Square made Simona think about Everett and Jones Barbeque. Truthfully, she could go for some of those ribs.

"Whatever Simona wants to do is fine with me," Donovan answered.

"I've got a taste for some barbecue from Everett and Jones," Simona said.

"Then that's what we'll do," he said.

They had to park a block away and wait half an hour, but the first bite of her ribs made it all worth it.

When they were settled, Donovan asked, "What happened, Simona? Why are you pulling away?"

She set her jar of lemonade down and blew out a long breath. "I saw the picture of us from Sheila's concert. I can't do this."

He reached across the table for her hand. "Sweetheart, why didn't you tell me? No one could recognize you in that picture. And even if they could, didn't I tell you I'd protect you? You're going to have to trust me. I need you to trust me."

"I hear you, Donovan, and I'm trying. I just don't think—"

"Let's just take it as it comes," he interrupted. "Can we do that?" He squeezed her hand reassuringly.

"I'll try."

"That's all I'm asking, baby."

Donovan observed Simona all through dinner and as they walked around Jack London Square. She seemed to have relaxed somewhat after talking, but he still sensed her hesitancy. He was so in love with this woman he couldn't see straight, and he allowed himself a moment to imagine what it would be like to come home to her—and Yasmine— every night. He chuckled inwardly, thinking about how fast the little girl had managed to wiggle herself deep within his heart. Simona's voice reclaimed his attention.

"Have you been to Oakland before?"

"A few times. Last time was two years ago when Terrence performed here and in San Francisco. That's where he met Janae." They stopped to stare out over the water.

"I remember Janae mentioning that. They seem really happy."

"They are. Terrence loves Janae and Nadia so much that he would do anything for them," he said, holding her eyes. Simona didn't reply, but he could tell she was thinking about what he said. He slung his arm around her shoulders, and they continued their walk.

"Simona? Is that you?" someone called out from nearby.

Donovan felt Simona stiffen in his arms.

Simona turned. "Amber."

"Hey. Um…I thought that was you. How've you been?"

"Fine. How's the acting going?"

Amber's gaze darted between him and Simona. "It's going good," she answered with a nervous chuckle. "I've done a few commercials, and I just landed a small part in a new television series. And I'll be going to New York next month." Amber paused. "So, um, are you back?"

"No. I'm just visiting my grandmother," Simona answered.

"Oh." Amber stuck her hand out to Donovan. "Hi, I'm Amber Rayne."

Donovan shook her hand. "Donovan Wright. Nice to meet you."

"Same here. Well, I'd better go." She gestured over her shoulder. "My friends are waiting. It was really good to see you, Simona. Maybe…maybe we can talk sometime. My number is the same."

Simona nodded.

Amber stood there a moment longer as if she wanted to say something else, but in the end turned and hurried off.

"What was that all about?" Donovan asked.

"Amber was my best friend and the one who introduced me to Travis. She was also one of the few who knew the truth about how and why we parted, and yet, when she was interviewed about our breakup, she lied so it wouldn't interfere with her career."

He brought her into the circle of his arms and kissed the top of her head. "I'm sorry, baby. You don't have to worry about that anymore."

"I know. It's just that we had been friends since elementary school."

Donovan nodded understandingly. "You ready to head back?"

"Yeah."

As soon as they arrived, Simona got Yasmine ready for bed. She came back to the family room where Donovan sat with Nana watching television and announced that she was going to take her shower. His gaze followed her until she was out of sight. She had been quiet since seeing Amber, and all he wanted to do was hold her in his arms.

"Did you two have a fight?" Nana asked.

Donovan turned and met her challenging stare. "No,

ma'am. She saw her friend, Amber, and I think it brought up some bad memories."

She eyed him for a moment. "Simona told you about that fiasco."

"Yes."

She pointed a finger his way. "My granddaughter went through a lot with that mess, and I won't stand for it again." She then proceeded to ask him about his job, what he thought about children and what his intentions were toward Simona.

So, this must be the overprotectiveness Simona warned me about. He answered her rapid-fire questions easily. "Nana, I love your granddaughter. I can assure you I will never hurt Simona *or* Yasmine," he said fiercely.

Nana leaned back in her chair, narrowed her eyes and scrutinized him with an intensity that would have made a lesser man turn tail and run. But Donovan's gaze didn't waver. He wanted her to see the truth in his words.

Finally, a slow smile spread across her lips. "I do believe my Simona has found herself a champion. All right, Donovan. You have my blessing."

He rose from his seat and hunkered down in front of her. Taking her hand, he said, "I promise to take good care of both my girls."

She patted his hand. "I like you, Donovan. Well, this old lady is going to bed. I have church in the morning and a dinner guest afterward."

He stood, helped her up and kissed her cheek. "Good night, Nana." Now alone, he shook his head. He thought his mother was bad. Donovan turned off the TV and the lights, then went to check on Simona. He knocked softly on her door.

Simona opened the door wearing a skimpy shorts set that exposed more than it covered, and he groaned. "You don't have anything else to sleep in?"

She smiled. "This is how I sleep in the summer." She stepped back so he could enter.

Donovan crossed the room and sat on the edge of the bed. His eyes strayed to Yasmine asleep in a crib on the other side of the room. He patted the bed. "Come here, sweetheart." He reached for her hand and entwined their fingers. "How're you doing?"

She released a deep sigh. "I'm okay. I honestly thought I had gotten over it, but I guess I'm still hurt by what Amber did."

"That's understandable. You were friends for a long time."

"I'll be fine."

"Oh, by the way, Nana and I had a nice talk."

Simona laughed softly. "In other words, she grilled you."

He nodded. "She did. She would make a helluva lawyer. But I had no problems with it. She loves you."

"What did you tell her?"

"The same thing I told you—that I'll be here for you."

She laid her head on his shoulder. "Thank you, Donovan."

"No thanks needed, baby." They sat in silence for several minutes then Donovan said, "I should probably leave now because I want to strip you naked and make you scream my name, and I don't want Nana to hear."

Her head popped up, and her mouth gaped open. "You are so outrageous."

"Me? I'm not the one who showed up at somebody's office with no panties on. I couldn't concentrate worth a damn all week."

Simona clapped a hand over her mouth to stifle a laugh. "But you enjoyed it?"

"You'd better believe it." He took her hand and placed it on the solid bulge in his pants. "See what you do to me? And cold showers for the past several days haven't helped."

"Aw, poor baby." She gave him a meaningful squeeze.

Donovan jumped up. "I'm going to bed."

She chuckled and stood. "Night."

He bent and kissed her. "See you in the morning."

Donovan headed for his room and another cold shower. Soon as they got home, it was going to be him, Simona and his bed.

Simona had been at work only two hours Tuesday morning when the nurse manager asked to see her. Mrs. Battle rarely summoned nurses to her office unless there was a problem. Simona hadn't had any trouble or complaints, so she had no idea why the woman wanted to see her. She knocked on the partially open door.

"Come in."

"Hi, Mrs. Battle. You wanted to see me?"

She stood. "Yes, Simona. Please close the door and have a seat."

The hairs on the back of her neck stood up, but she did as asked. "Is there a problem with my performance?"

She smiled briefly. "No, Simona. You're one of the most dedicated and compassionate nurses on staff." She gestured to a chair. "Please."

Simona perched on the edge of the chair and waited while Mrs. Battle walked over to a small conference table and retrieved what looked like a newspaper.

Mrs. Battle reclaimed her chair and clasped her hands together. "Something was brought to my attention this morning, and I wasn't sure you knew about it."

Simona's heart hammered in her chest. "I'm sorry. I'm not following."

"This," Mrs. Battle said, and handed her the paper.

She took the paper and unfolded it. What Simona thought was a newspaper was actually a tabloid magazine. She carefully unfolded it and froze. On the cover was a picture of her, Donovan and Yasmine at Lake Merritt last weekend. But what captured her attention was the large headline that read, From Actor to Record Label Executive: Simona Andrews Has Cornered the Entertainment Market. There was an old picture of her and Travis, something about a possible secret love child and a host of other things that she couldn't make sense of.

She gasped sharply. "No, no, no," she whispered. She tossed the magazine on the desk with shaky hands and clutched her chest, struggling to draw in a breath. Her stomach dropped, and her heart raced. Simona squeezed her eyes shut as a wave of dizziness washed over her. This could not be happening again.

"Simona?"

Her eyes snapped open.

"I take it you hadn't seen this."

Simona shook her head quickly.

Mrs. Battle came around the desk and sat in the other visitor chair next to Simona. "How about you tell me what's going on?"

Simona nodded, still not believing it was happening again. She shared the details of her relationship with Travis and their breakup, and those of her current relationship with Donovan. Mrs. Battle already knew the specifics surrounding Yasmine. "Is this going to cost me my job?" Simona asked shakily when she was done speaking.

The older woman shook her head. "Of course not. But you look like you could use some time off to deal with this." She squeezed Simona's hand reassuringly.

"Thank you. I think I'll take you up on your offer." Truthfully, she wouldn't be able to do her job anyway with all the emotions swirling around in the pit of her stomach. What was she going to do? She had just started to get comfortable in her new home, and now she faced the possibility of having to move again.

Chapter 18

Donovan divided his gaze between the three people around the table. What was supposed to be a working lunch had turned into a Q & A session about his love life.

"Oh, come on, Donovan. Don't keep me in suspense. I like Simona," Audrey said.

Terrence folded his arms and laughed. "I have to say I'm enjoying watching you squirm the way you did me."

"And as I said before, I'm not running like you were," Donovan said. He turned to face Brad. "Do you have something to say?"

Brad held up his hands in mock surrender. "No way. The last time I said something, it ended with my wife calling me dense and giving me the silent treatment for six hours."

They all laughed, recalling the incident right after Terrence and Janae met. Brad had assumed that Janae was another booty call before he knew the truth. Donovan turned back to Audrey. "Yes, Audrey, I'm in love with Simona."

"Ooh, goodie! I heard she has a little girl."

He reached into his pocket for his cell and brought up the photo of himself and Yasmine that he couldn't resist taking on her birthday. "Her name is Yasmine, and she just turned one." Donovan passed the phone to Audrey. "She's actually Simona's niece. Simona's sister and her sister's fiancé were killed in a car accident."

"That's so sad." Audrey adjusted the phone so Brad could see. "She's adorable, Donovan. Look at those little ponytails and that big smile. She has a head full of hair. And you look like a natural holding her. Brad and I have been talking. And since I can't have children, we're thinking of adopting."

"That's great," Donovan said.

"I get first dibs on godfather," Terrence said, reaching for the phone. They all laughed. "She's a beautiful little girl. She and Nadia need to meet." He held the phone out to Donovan. "I bet you were a goner the first time you held her and she turned those bright eyes on you. That's what happened to me with Nadia."

Donovan stared at the picture, remembering the night Yasmine was sick. "Yeah, man. She stole my heart. Anyway, isn't this supposed to be a working lunch?" His cell rang as he was putting it back in his pocket. He didn't recognize the number on the display. "Let me get this."

"Hello. May I please speak to Donovan Wright?" It was a female voice he didn't recognize.

He frowned. "Speaking."

"Donovan, this is Frances Walker, Simona's grandmother."

"Nana? Is everything okay?" he asked with concern. He had given her his number with instructions to call if she ever needed anything.

"I don't think so."

"Are you sick? Do I need to find Simona?"

"It's not me." She paused. "It's Simona. My neighbor brought me one of those trash magazines, and there's a picture of you, Simona and Yasmine at Lake Merritt on the cover."

Donovan's heart pounded in fear, and he didn't realize he was standing until he took a step. "What are you talking about?"

"Honey, I need you to get to my baby." Her voice broke. "I don't think she can take this a second time."

"Does she know about it?"

Terrence rose from his chair and mouthed, "What's going on?"

Donovan held up a finger.

Nana continued. "Yes. I called to warn her, and she told me that someone at her job had given the paper to her manager. The woman is going to let her take some time off. Donovan, I'm afraid of what she might be thinking. She loves her job and…"

"Nana, don't you worry. I'm leaving right now. I promised you I wouldn't let anything happen to her, and I won't. As soon as I find out how she is, I'll call you."

"Thank you."

"You don't have to thank me. Now, I need you to stay calm and try not to worry. I'll take care of her and Yasmine." He completed the call and paced. He was going to kill somebody. Who would do something like this? No one even knew she'd been home…except Amber.

"What's going on, D?" Terrence asked anxiously.

"That was Simona's grandmother. Remember what I told you about Simona's ex?"

"The wannabe actor?"

"Yeah. Apparently, while we were in Oakland this past weekend, someone took a picture of us and it's on the front cover of a tabloid. I need to get my hands on that article, then I'm going to get Simona and take her and Yasmine to my house. After that, I might be needing bail money."

Audrey stood. "I'm on that article. I know someone in publicity who can get their hands on it in a matter of minutes from the paper's website."

Brad clapped him on the shoulder. "Let me know when you're ready to make a statement. I'm going to get to the bottom of this and find out what your legal rights are." He sailed out behind Audrey.

"What do you need me to do, Donovan?" Terrence asked.

"Can I borrow the SUV so I can take Yasmine's crib to my house?"

"I'll do you one better. I'm coming with you." Terrence hit the intercom. "Mrs. Lewis, we have an emergency. Donovan and I will be out of the office for the rest of the afternoon. Please reschedule any appointments."

"No problem."

"I'll be in your office in two minutes. Let me call Janae and tell her what's going on."

Donovan nodded and rushed to his office. Audrey came in right behind him with the magazine.

"Donovan, it's not good."

He scanned the headline and the picture. Inside, he quickly read the article. *Secret love child?* His jaw tightened.

"If you need anything, call me," Audrey said, rubbing his arm in a comforting manner. "I plan to make sure Brad sues everybody from the person who started those lies and everybody who made a comment to the magazine, to the stores that carry this trash."

"Thanks." He grabbed his jacket, met Terrence in the hallway and the two men raced out of the office.

Eve met him at the door holding Yasmine.

"Hey, Eve. Where's Simona?"

"Hi. She got here about thirty minutes ago and went

straight to her room. She's been crying, and even Yasmine senses something's wrong."

Donovan reached for Yasmine. "Come here, angel. You worried about your mama?" He kissed her temple. "Don't worry. I'll take care of her. Eve, this is Terrence Campbell. Terrence, Eve, Simona's neighbor."

"Oh, this man needs no introduction," Eve said with a smile. "I love your music. It's nice to meet you."

"Thanks, and same here," Terrence said.

"Eve, can you pack up some of Yasmine's things? I'm going to take them home with me. Terrence will help you."

"Of course. Let me take her."

He left them to their task and knocked on Simona's door. "Simona, it's me. Can I come in?" When she didn't answer, he tried the knob and found the door unlocked. He peeked in and spotted her curled up on the bed. His heart broke. Closing the door behind him, he kicked off his shoes and eased onto the bed, pulling her into his arms. For a few minutes, he just held her. "Hey, sweetheart. It's been a pretty rough day, huh?"

"I have to leave. I can't do this again, Donovan. I've tried so hard to do the right thing," Simona cried.

"No, you don't and you won't. You and Yasmine are going to hang out at my house for a few days until this blows over. Eve's packing up Yasmine's things, and Terrence is here with his truck to carry her crib."

She lifted her tearstained eyes to his. "I can't do that. What about your job?"

"I don't care about my job right now. It'll wait. You're far more important to me. So I want you to pack your stuff."

"But—"

"No buts, baby. I love you, and I promise I'll take care of this."

Her eyes widened. "What did you say?"

Caressing her face, he repeated himself. "I said I love you, and I will take care of this mess."

She angled her head as if trying to process his words, then finally agreed.

Donovan sat up. "I'll wait for you out front. I'm going to see if Terrence needs help." He kissed her tenderly. "It's going to be all right, Simona."

"Okay," she said in a small voice.

He took a moment to call Nana on his way to help his friend load the truck. It hurt him to see Simona like this, and it was all he could do not to hop on a plane and track Amber down. Whoever had done this would pay, and pay dearly.

Simona took in the immaculate yards and expensive homes on the street as Donovan turned into a driveway with a three-car garage. He pressed a button, and two of the doors began to rise. Terrence backed his SUV halfway into one, and Donovan drove into the other one.

"I'll get you settled, then help Terrence unload."

"I can help."

"We can manage."

He got out and came around to her side. She slowly emerged from the car and gathered Yasmine from the backseat. Instead of going through the garage, he led her around to the front door and stood back to let her enter. Her eyes widened as she entered a large foyer with marble flooring.

Simona took in her surroundings as she followed Donovan down the hall. She noted formal living and dining areas across from where they entered, which she assumed was the family room. The deep tans and browns throughout gave a definite masculine feel to the house. Although the furniture was expensive, the atmosphere still felt homey. The walls held two landscape pieces similar to the ones she had seen at Terrence and Janae's house, and she wondered if the same artist had done them. Donovan's voice interrupted her thoughts.

"Make yourself comfortable."

"You have a beautiful house. How long have you lived here?"

"Three years. I got tired of hearing doors slam and feet pounding on the stairs at all hours of the night when I lived in my condo. I found that I like the peace and quiet."

She laughed. "I remember the same thing in my apartment." Simona pointed to one of the paintings. "This is spectacular. Where did you get it?"

"Janae painted both of them. I bought them when she had her first gallery showing a year ago."

"Wow."

"Yeah. She does amazing work. I'm going to help Terrence. Feel free to explore, and don't worry about Yasmine breaking anything."

"You say that now."

He smiled and tweaked Yasmine's nose on the way out.

"Donovan," she called after him. He stopped and turned. "Thank you."

"You're welcome."

Simona took one more glance around. "Let's go check this place out, Yasmine." The rest of the house was just as spectacular. She counted four bedrooms, a weight room and five bathrooms. Her favorite room by far was the kitchen. It had to be almost three times the size of her small one and contained every gadget a professional chef would need. She chuckled, remembering that Donovan didn't know how to cook well, and wondered why he had bought a house with such a large kitchen.

After their tour, she and Yasmine sat in the family room and waited for Donovan. Simona had to constantly chase Yasmine around to keep her from destroying the room. "He definitely needs some childproofing," she mumbled.

She found a toy in one of the bags Donovan brought in that held the little girl's attention.

Leaning back on the couch, she thought about Donovan confessing to loving her. She remembered him saying it that night in his office, and at the time, she hadn't thought he meant it. Today, his words left no doubt in her mind. But now she had to deal with this mess. She tried to figure out how someone found out about her and Donovan. Even more puzzling was why he or she felt the need to start more rumors.

It had been over a year since she had seen Travis, so what would he have to gain by making that crazy statement about her being the type of woman to use a child to get money? She racked her brain trying to come up with a reason. Simona bolted upright. "Amber," she whispered. But why? Amber had apparently moved on with her life and gotten everything she wanted in her career.

Simona retrieved her cell phone from her purse and scrolled until she came to the number she had never deleted. Taking a deep breath, she tapped the screen.

"Amber? It's Simona."

"Oh, my God, Simona. I'm-so-sorry-I-didn't-do-this-I-know-you-think-I-did-but-I-didn't-I-promise."

The words came out in a tearful jumbled mess before Simona could say anything.

"Amber, you're the only one I saw when I was home. If you didn't, who did?"

Amber sniffed. "I don't know. I know I messed up the first time, and I lost my best friend. But I *swear* it wasn't me."

Simona didn't know what to believe. "Did you talk to anyone? What about the people you were with?"

"It was just a group of us celebrating mine and a couple of others' success. Oh, no."

"What, Amber?"

"Lorna showed up a few minutes after I saw you."

Simona sighed wearily and scrubbed a hand across her forehead. Lorna Price had been interested in Travis and upset when he chose Simona over her. "What did you tell her?"

"I didn't tell her anything. One of the other girls asked me who you were, and she might've overheard me talking. I'm so, so sorry, Simona."

"But what would she have to gain by dragging my name through the mud? Travis and I have been over for more than a year."

"She's still bitter and she hasn't been getting many parts, whereas Travis's career has taken off. I knew she blamed you, but that was a long time ago. I don't even know who invited her. We don't talk anymore. Not since…"

"I have to go," Simona said softly. She didn't give Amber a chance to reply.

"Mamamama."

She picked up her baby and hugged her tight. "Mommy's not going to let anyone come near you." And she was Yasmine's mother, the one who vowed to guard her with the ferociousness of a lioness protecting her cubs. Simona couldn't go through that circus again, and she would do whatever it took to keep that from happening, even if it meant leaving.

Her heart squeezed. To keep her little girl safe, she would leave everything behind. And everyone.

Chapter 19

Donovan lowered his body into his chair and buried his head in his hands. Over the past week, the media frenzy besieging him and Simona had tested his control in ways he'd never imagined. He was wound so tight that the least little thing might make him snap.

Brad had finally made some headway on the several lawsuits he was filing and had demanded a retraction be printed, but he also had some disturbing news. Thanks to Amber, they found out that the person who initially provided the false information was a woman linked to Simona's ex. Under pressure, the woman had admitted to following them and taking pictures.

The one person Donovan wanted to lay hands on, however, was Travis Jacobs. The arrogant asshole was still trying to use Simona to make himself look good in the media by adding to the lies and claiming that Simona was the type of person to use a child for blackmail. But when

Donovan finished with Travis, his looks were likely to be the only thing he had left.

The only time he felt some measure of peace was when he went home. The delightful laughter and kisses that Yasmine greeted him with, and the soul-stirring lovemaking with Simona that filled his nights, gave him a sense of completion and fulfillment unlike anything he had ever felt. Donovan finally understood what Terrence had tried to explain after he married Janae and had Nadia.

But for the past two days, Simona seemed to be withdrawing, and every time he tried to talk to her, she would tell him she was fine. In his heart he knew she wasn't, and he hoped with time she would open up to him. The constant hype in the tabloids and on the entertainment TV shows was taking a toll on her. He had done everything in his power to prove to her that he'd kept his promises. It was up to her to believe him. Only now he had to call and tell her that Travis wanted a paternity test.

Taking a deep breath, he picked up the phone. "Hey, sweetheart," he said when Simona answered. He could hear Yasmine in the background babbling.

"Hey. Is something wrong?"

"Brad has gotten the magazine to print a retraction, and Lorna confessed to following us and taking the pictures."

"Oh, thank goodness. Now I can finally put this mess behind me."

"Simona, there's something else… Travis is requesting a paternity test."

"*What*? He knows this baby is not his," she hissed.

"I know that, too. It's clear he's still trying to keep his fifteen minutes of fame by lying. But taking the test will put him out of our lives for good."

"Donovan, I don't want to subject Yasmine to this drama."

"You won't have to. The only information Travis will

receive from the testing is that the baby is not his, nothing more. You can take Yasmine to the hospital today to get it done. I can meet you there. The sooner we get this done, the sooner we can move on."

Silence reigned for a full minute before she finally agreed.

Later he met her at the hospital for the test, then they spent a quiet evening together. Donovan went to work the following day feeling confident that in a few short days it would all be over. He met with Terrence to discuss two concert dates in New York and New Jersey, then the two of them met with a prospective client. He took a moment to check on Simona, and she sounded better.

Donovan attended his meeting with the A and R department later that afternoon, then called it a day. He was anxious to get home to his girls. The delicious scent of food hit his nose as soon as he entered the house through the garage and made his stomach growl. He smiled and waited for the familiar footsteps.

The seconds ticked off, and his smile faded. He walked through the quiet house. It had taken him less than a day to get accustomed to not being alone, and the sounds were noticeably absent.

He climbed the stairs and called out to Simona, but got no answer. The pace of his heart accelerated when he found several things missing from the room Yasmine was using. Donovan burst into his bedroom and snatched open dresser drawers and the closet and found Simona's things gone. Dread settled in his belly, and he sprinted back downstairs to the kitchen. On his way to the garage, a sheet of paper on the refrigerator that he hadn't noticed before caught his attention. He removed it and read:

Donovan, I can't take it anymore and I apologize for the stress this has caused you on your job. I think it

would be better for both of us if I left, so you can get on with your life. Please forgive me for bringing my past to your doorstep. Yasmine and I will be fine, and know that I will always love you.
Simona

He let out a frustrated growl, then braced his hands on the counter and bowed his head. He'd thought they were good. Pain settled in his chest and swelled to massive proportions in a matter of seconds. "I can't let her go. I have to find her."

He slammed his hand on the counter and whipped out his phone. His call to Simona's cell immediately went to voicemail, and the one to her home went unanswered. He tried her grandmother, but Nana hadn't heard from her, either. Where could she be?

No matter where she had gone, he was going to find her and bring her back where she belonged…with him.

"Believe me, Eve," Simona said as she added more clothes to the suitcase, "I've thought about everything you're saying, but I just can't do this anymore. And Donovan…" She dropped down on the bed and swiped at a tear. "He's been so amazing through all this, but I see what it's doing to him—the way he's had to fight the media, the stress it's putting on his job—I can't do this to him. Didn't you see the latest headline that said Donovan and I were trying to pass the baby off as Travis's to extort money?" It had been hard to leave Donovan's house, but sitting in her bedroom now, Simona felt she had made the right decision.

Eve sighed. "Yes, I saw it. But Simona, honey, Donovan loves you, and I'm sure he's more concerned with *your* stress level. You don't have to leave. You know that paternity test is going to come back negative. From what I can see, Donovan must be doing something, because I saw a retraction printed in that first tabloid and I'm sure the others will follow."

"And in the meantime, his spotless reputation is being dragged through the mud." She stood, zipped the suitcase and took it out to the car. Eve was sitting on the couch when she returned. "I think that about does it. I really appreciate you letting me stay at your house."

"I told you before, you're welcome to use it for as long as you need. I already called my caretaker, and she'll be waiting for you. Call me and let me know you arrived safely." Eve bounced Yasmine in her arms. "Auntie Eve is going to miss you, baby cakes." She kissed and hugged Yasmine.

Simona did one more walk-through to make sure she hadn't forgotten anything. Satisfied, she locked up. She strapped Yasmine into her car seat and faced Eve. "Well, this is it." She handed her the house keys.

Eve had tears in her eyes. "I'm going to miss you. I'll make sure the house is taken care of until you come back. And I know you will." She gave Simona a strong hug. "Be safe, and don't forget to call me."

Wiping her tears, Simona said, "I won't." They shared another emotional hug and parted. Minutes later she was on Interstate 5 heading south to San Diego.

She missed Donovan already, and several times during the drive the tears started again. She had to pull over once because she was crying so hard she couldn't see the road. Fortunately, Yasmine slept most of the way.

Two and a half hours later, she parked in the driveway of a house on a corner lot with a wide covered porch holding a cushioned loveseat and two matching chairs with a small table between them. She blew out a long breath and felt some of the tension start to drain.

The front door opened just as Simona stuck the key in the lock. "Hello."

A dark-skinned older woman with salt-and-pepper hair

cut in short layers smiled warmly. "You must be Simona. Come in and unburden yourself. My name is Marlena. Eve told me about your little one. I took the liberty of having my son bring over my grandson's crib for you to use." She walked while she talked. "So you can lay her in here. I put on some fresh sheets."

"Thank you, Miss Marlena." Simona placed Yasmine in the crib and covered her with the sheet. She turned the lamp down to the lowest setting and followed Marlena on a tour of the three-bedroom house. She tried to pay attention to the woman's lively chatter, but fatigue set in and she had a hard time keeping her eyes open. Marlena must have noticed.

"You must be exhausted, child, and I'm just going on and on. Let's get your things in so you can rest."

"Oh, you don't have to do that. I can manage on my own."

Marlena waved Simona off. "Nonsense. Now, come on."

Not having the strength to argue, Simona followed, and they emptied the car in no time. Simona thanked her, and Marlena told Simona she would be by tomorrow. She trudged down the hall to the bedroom next to the one where Yasmine slept and took out her phone to call Eve. There were three messages from Donovan that she had missed when she turned the phone off. She spoke to Eve briefly, hung up and listened to the messages.

Simona, baby, where are you? Please pick up.

Simona, please call me. I need to know you're all right.

Tears blurred her vision.

Simona, I know this has been hard. Please come back. You don't have to fight alone. I'll be right by your side. I love you and need you here with me. Kiss Yasmine for me. Know that I will not stop fighting for us.

She held the phone against her heart and curled up in a fetal position on the bed as deep, wrenching sobs tore from her throat. Simona had no idea how long she lay there before she mustered up enough strength to shower and crawl beneath the covers for the night.

The next morning her head felt as if it weighed a ton, her throat was raw from crying and her eyes were bloodshot and puffy. With supreme effort, she dragged herself out of bed and went to make oatmeal. Yasmine was already awake and would be ready to eat soon, especially since she had fallen asleep so early.

After she fed Yasmine and forced down half of a banana herself, Simona went out to the porch. She sat in one of the chairs and placed the little girl on her lap. She marveled at the beauty in front of her. Eve's house was close enough to the ocean for her to have a small, distant view. Here, she didn't have to worry about being hounded by the media and hearing the gossip on TV. Mrs. Battle had approved a six-week emergency leave, and that gave Simona time to decide her next move.

A flock of birds flew by, and Yasmine tried to squirm out of Simona's lap to see where they went. Simona stood and walked to the edge of the porch so the little girl could see them. She pointed. "Birds. Can you say birds?" Yasmine said something and pointed. Simona laughed and kissed her. "That's right, birds. You are such a smart girl."

"Dadadada."

She went still. This was the third time Yasmine had said it. The first time had been when they were at her grandmother's house. Deacon Mitchell had come to dinner and mistakenly assumed Donovan was her father—a fact that Donovan never denied—and said, "Go to your daddy." The man had thought it cute when she repeated it several times. The second time had been when Donovan came home from work one evening. The emotion that had filled his face had moved Simona to tears. He didn't put her down for the rest of the evening.

A fresh wave of tears crested her eyes. Donovan probably missed Yasmine as much as she missed him...as much as they both missed him. But this was for the best, Simona assured herself. She couldn't let him sacrifice all his hard work for her mistake.

Donovan was at his wit's end by Friday. It had been three days since Simona left, and he hadn't heard one word, though he'd left several messages. It was driving him crazy. The silence in his house was deafening, and his bed was cold and lonely. In the short time they'd been together, he had gotten used to Simona snuggling next to him or lying half on top of him to sleep. And Yasmine. God, how he missed her. She had even said "Dada." He'd give anything to have his girls back. He needed them to make his life complete.

"Any word from Simona?" Terrence stuck his head in the door.

"No, and I'm about to lose my mind. T, I love her," Donovan said emotionally. "I don't know what I'll do if I don't find her."

"I'll help in any way I can. I have some good news. I just talked to Brad, and he told me he contacted Travis Jacobs's lawyer. Apparently, Travis is willing to say he made a mistake about asking for the paternity test."

Donovan rose to his feet swiftly. "Mistake!" he yelled. "That punk didn't make a mistake. He *knew* the baby wasn't his."

"Calm down and let me finish," Terrence said.

He unclenched his fists and drew in several angry breaths.

"Brad told the lawyer that unless his client came clean, he would drag Travis to court and make sure the media gets a front row seat. He would make Simona look like Mother Teresa, which isn't a far stretch, and let the public decide.

The implications for Travis's career would be monumental." Terrence chuckled. "Brad is flying to Oakland on Monday to meet with him. The lawyer wants to settle out of court. Just so you know, he's filing libel and defamation of character suits for both you and Simona, including the mess from the first time. And because Mr. Idiot decided to say the same thing in an interview, Brad's throwing in slander. He's already trying to subpoena the tape."

"Good. I hope Travis decides on the right course of action."

"Just let Brad handle it. The last thing you need is an assault charge."

"As I recall, you knocked out Janae's ex for far less."

Terrence nodded. "It felt good, too. Well, maybe one good punch. I've got your back." They did a fist bump.

Donovan allowed himself a small smile. "Always. I think I'm going to leave. I want to stop by Eve's house and see if she knows where Simona is. She wasn't home when I went over yesterday."

"Let me know if you need me to do anything. Why don't you take Monday off, too? Monique can handle things, and I'll be here."

"Thanks, bro. I'll let you know if I hear anything."

Donovan drove to Simona's house and parked out front. Her car wasn't there, and it looked as though no one had been there for several days. He got out, walked across the street and rang Eve's doorbell, gazing over the neighborhood while he waited. *Please let her be home.* He spun around when the door opened.

"Donovan," she said with surprise.

"Hi, Eve. May I come in for a few minutes?"

"Sure." She led him to the living room and offered him a seat. "Can I get you anything?"

"No, thanks. I just need to know if you have any idea

where Simona went." Something like guilt flashed in her face. "Eve, please. I need to find her."

She took the chair next to his and sighed heavily. "I tried to convince her to stay, but she was hell-bent on leaving."

"Did she tell you where she was going? I've been out of my mind worrying about her and Yasmine." He got up, paced the room and came back. He squatted down in front of her. "Eve, I'm desperate. I love Simona and I love Yasmine. I'm begging you, please, please tell me where she is."

"Lord, if my husband had ever looked at me this way or shown half the concern you're showing, we wouldn't be divorced today. She's at my vacation home in San Diego."

Donovan pulled Eve from her chair and engulfed her in a hug. "Thank you, thank you," he whispered.

She wiped a tear from the corner of her eye. "I'll get you the address." She came back with a piece of paper with an address and a phone number, and pressed it into his hand. "I'm glad she has you. My number is on there. Call me and let me know how she's doing. I know this has been hard for you, too. How are you holding up?"

"I'll be fine once I have her back. Thanks, Eve. I'll call you."

He got in his car and offered up a silent prayer of thanks. Donovan really wanted to get on the road now, but it was already after three, and with the traffic, it would take him as long to get there as it would if he left a few hours from now. Besides, he was so anxious that there was no way he could sit through hours of traffic. He went home, packed and reserved a room at a hotel in San Diego for two nights. Then he called Terrence to give him an update and mention that he might need to be off longer.

Donovan gassed up and was on the road by seven. There was still a fair amount of traffic, and the normal two-hour drive was extended to three. He drove to the address Eve had written down and parked across the street. He saw a light on and was tempted to knock on the door tonight. He stifled the urge, started the car and went to his hotel.

Later, while flipping through the television channels, his stomach growled and reminded him that he had skipped dinner. He had been so determined to get to San Diego that food was the last thing on his mind. Now, however, his appetite had returned with a vengeance, and he needed to find some food. He laced up his tennis shoes, stuffed his wallet and room key into his pocket and clicked off the TV. Donovan stopped at the front desk to ask the clerk for some late-night food suggestions and ended up at a nearby bar and grill. He ordered a bacon cheeseburger with french fries and a beer.

While eating, he thought about how Simona would react when she saw him. Would she be happy, or would she stand by the words she'd left in the note, that it was better if she left and they got on with their lives? Whose life would be better? Certainly not his. He had been absolutely miserable without her. Donovan found himself reaching for her in the middle of the night or getting up to check on Yasmine, only to find an empty crib. No matter how long it took, he was not returning home without Simona.

Without her, he didn't have a home.

Chapter 20

The next day, Simona finished packing her beach bag, picked up Yasmine and went outside to put her in the stroller. "Okay, sweetie. Let's go check out the ocean." She glanced up at the cloudless blue sky and smiled. Summer was almost over, with September right around the corner, and the temperatures hovered around eighty degrees.

It was a perfect day for the three-block walk to the beach. Apparently everyone else had decided to spend Saturday morning the same way. She strolled leisurely down the street, responding to greetings from passersby and stopping to point out the birds, Yasmine's new favorite pastime.

She found a spot on the crowded beach near the sidewalk because she had no desire to try to push the stroller across the sand. Simona spread the blanket on the sand, sat down, then stood Yasmine up. At the first touch of sand on the little girl's soles, she clung to Simona and lifted her feet. Simona laughed. "You don't like the sand? It's okay. See?" Simona demonstrated by putting her feet in the sand and drizzling the powdery substance over them. She poured some on Yasmine's feet, and gradually, after a few minutes, Yasmine was kicking her feet in the sand on her own.

The past four days had been exactly what Simona needed. Everything was perfect—well, not everything. Thoughts of Donovan dominated the space in her brain at all hours of the day and night, and last night she woke up to reach for him, only to find an empty spot. It had taken her one night in his arms to know she wanted to wake up every morning with him. How was he doing? Was the talk dying down now that she was gone so he could get back to his life?

She had been tempted to watch one of the entertainment shows or do an internet search, but she didn't want to see another lie written about her. She still got angry when she thought about Travis attacking her character. The only thing stopping her from suing his butt was the fact that it would mean more time with the media in her face, and she'd had enough to last two lifetimes.

"No, no. You can't eat the sand, baby." She caught Yasmine's hand.

They had lunch and stayed for another hour, then packed up for the walk home. The sun was directly overhead, and Simona picked up her pace. Her steps slowed as she approached Eve's house, and her heart rate kicked up when she spotted a familiar figure sprawled in a chair on the porch. He stood as she turned up the walkway, and her breath caught. The sight of him never failed to make her pulse race and her body heat up.

"Donovan. What are you doing here?" For a moment, he just stood there staring at her with a yearning in his eyes that sucked her in by degrees.

"I came for you."

Yasmine tried her best to climb out of the stroller to get to him. Finally, Simona undid the strap and set her on her feet. She ran to him as fast as her little legs would carry her.

"Dadada."

Donovan squatted down and scooped her up as soon as Yasmine was in reach, placing happy kisses all over her face. "How's my baby girl? I missed you." He hugged and kissed her, and Yasmine held on for dear life.

Seeing the happy reunion and the tears standing in Donovan's eyes filled Simona's heart with emotion, and she fought back her own tears. He came to where she stood and brushed her cheek with the back of his hand. Her eyes slid closed from the sweetness of his touch.

"And how's my other baby girl?"

He leaned down and captured her mouth in a kiss so achingly tender the tears spilled from her eyes and ran freely down her face. "I'm okay."

"Why did you leave me?"

"We can talk inside."

Donovan tried to put Yasmine down so he could carry the stroller up the steps, but she put up a fuss and wouldn't let go of his shirt. "I'm just going to put the stroller on the porch. It'll be one minute." But she wasn't having it.

"I got it," Simona said. Once they were inside, she left the stroller near the door so she could take it back outside to clean out all the sand and not track it all over the floors. "Um, do you want something to eat or drink?"

"Nah, I'm fine. The only thing I want right now is to hold you in my arms. Can I hold you, Simona?"

His husky plea melted her insides, and she rushed into his free arm. He held her so tight she could barely breathe, but right now she didn't care.

"I missed you so much, sweetheart. I was out of my

mind, wondering where you were and if you were all right. Don't leave me again."

She backed out of his arms. "I ca...can't go back."

"Yes, you can. The tabloid printed a retraction, and we're handling Travis and that Lorna woman. You don't have to fight alone anymore, Simona. I promised to protect you, and I will if you let me."

"Donovan, you can't protect me from everyone."

"Want to bet? Stop running, baby. Don't let them win. Together we can beat this. Trust me. Trust *us*."

She wanted so badly to trust him, but every negative word she had read in those articles flashed through her mind, the memories taunting her. "I can't," she whispered. "What if this messes up your career? The public's perception of you is part of your job."

Donovan closed the distance and wrapped his arm around her. "Sweetheart, I'm not worried about those lies, and you shouldn't be either. The people I work with know me and don't believe everything they read."

"But what if it does? I'll never be able to forgive myself." She wouldn't be able to bear seeing contempt in his eyes.

He narrowed his eyes. "You can't be thinking I'll blame you." He reached up to pull Yasmine's fingers out of his mouth.

Simona nodded. "You say you don't now, but what if this shows up again later? I couldn't take it if you—"

"Don't even think it," he said, cutting her off. "I will never resent or hate you. This is *not* your fault, Simona." He sighed heavily. "Baby, don't do this."

"I have to. I have to think about Yasmine and how it'll affect her."

He shook his head. "More excuses. Be honest. All of these are cover-ups for the real problem. What are you afraid of?"

She opened her mouth to say she wasn't afraid, but

closed it. Simona was afraid—afraid of how her colleagues would perceive her and afraid that she would lose the job she had come to love. But mostly she was afraid he would—despite what he said—wake up one morning, say that this was all her fault and walk away. Yasmine started whining and rubbing her eyes. "I think she's getting tired. It's time for her nap." Simona extended her arms.

Donovan moved the baby out of her reach. "She's fine, and you didn't answer my question. What are you afraid of?"

"Donovan..."

He shook his head. "Answer the question."

"Fine. I'm afraid my coworkers are going to think I'm this gold-digging slut," she blurted. "I'm afraid that I'm going to lose my job. And I'm afraid that one day, even though you said you wouldn't, you'll resent all the drama I've caused you and leave," she finished on a broken sob.

"In other words, you don't trust me," he said resignedly. "I've done everything to show you that I'm a man of my word, that you can trust me. I love you, Simona, but I don't know what else to do."

"I need time."

"Where's Yasmine's room?"

She pointed, and he turned and walked away.

He came back a few minutes later and said, "I'll see you later."

Simona stood in the middle of the room, her heart breaking into a million pieces. Why couldn't she let go? She loved him so much it hurt.

Donovan came back later to see Yasmine and tuck her in for the night. He hardly said two words to Simona, and she grasped just how much she had hurt him. He left without kissing her goodbye and did the same thing the next day. Simona stood off to the side observing him playing with Yasmine and hearing her happy screams. When she came outside to the porch and found Donovan stretched out on the couch with Yasmine on his chest, both of them asleep, Simona nearly lost it. She couldn't give this man up. But she feared it was too late.

An hour later, Donovan brought Yasmine inside and laid her in the crib. He returned to the living room and sat on the sofa next to Simona. For the longest time, he just sat there. Finally, without looking her way, he said, "I've given you time, Simona, and I've decided that I'm going to do whatever it takes to get you to trust me." He shifted to face her. "You might as well stop running because wherever you go, I will find you. From now on, there's only one place you'll ever need to run to, and that's my arms."

He came to his feet, pulled an envelope from his pocket and placed it on the coffee table in front of them. "I'll see you later."

Simona sat stunned and confused. He wasn't giving up on them. Then why did he leave? She stared at the envelope, almost afraid to open it. But curiosity got the best of her, and she slid her finger under the flap and took out the folded piece of paper. At first she thought he had typed a letter, but realized it was a copy of lyrics to a song.

It's Only You
[V 1]
From the day we met, I always knew
You would be the one to change my world.
Whether it's your charming, sexy smile or that thing you do,
Your love whispers with a voice of what's lasting and true.
[Chorus]
It's only you who sets my soul on fire.
You're my one desire.
I'll be loving you only till the end of time.
From this day forward, you will always be mine.

[V 2]
Your love fills the empty spaces and makes me
whole.
It deepens the joy and peace in my soul.
In your arms it's like I'm being loved for the first
time,
And my heart belongs to you for a lifetime.
[Repeat Chorus]
[Bridge]
No matter how the winds blow
Or how cold the nights may be,
From now on there's only you, only me
Because
[Repeat Chorus x2]
Fade

She recognized his bold handwriting below the printed
lyrics: *I penned these words years ago, but only now do
I know that they were meant for you. Always have been.*

Penned them years ago? Meant for her? Simona scrambled off the couch and went to the kitchen table where her
laptop sat. She turned it on and searched the internet for the
title. "You've got to be kidding me." There were thousands
of hits. Then a memory sparked. She typed in Monte's
name, and a YouTube video link popped up. She clicked
on it and turned the volume up. Monte's sexy baritone filtered through the speakers. She picked up the paper, and
her heart beat faster. *Donovan wrote this song.*

Another memory surfaced. The platinum record on his
wall was for this incredible song. A female voice sang
the second verse. Simona closed her eyes and focused
on the words. She replayed it again and again, listening
to the soulful ballad and letting the words seep into her
heart. He said the words were meant for her and always
had been. She grabbed her cell.

"Donovan, I love you and I'm so sorry," she said as soon as he picked up. "I trust you, and I know you keep your promises. I don't want to give you up, either. I'm not running anymore. I want to run to you." He was silent. "Donovan?"

"Then run to me, baby."

She whirled around to see him standing in the doorway with his arms outstretched. She dropped the phone and flew into his arms. He grabbed her up with such force that she thought he might crack her spine. Simona was crying and kissing him and telling him how much she loved him. He laughed and spun her around until she was dizzy.

"I love you, Simona Andrews."

"And I love you, Donovan Wright." She lowered her head and kissed him, attempting to infuse it with everything she felt and couldn't express.

Donovan lay on the bed waiting for Simona while she tucked Yasmine in. There were no words to describe the joy he was feeling.

"Hey."

He sat up. "Hey, yourself. Is Yasmine asleep?"

"She's out like a light."

"Good. Come here, baby." He pulled her to stand between his legs and settled his hands at her waist. "You're always taking care of everyone, so tonight I want to take care of you. I'm going to run you a nice, hot bubble bath, and then I'm going to give you a full body massage. Afterward, I'm going to make love to you long and slow. How does that sound?"

"Mmm, it sounds wonderful."

Donovan undid the buttons on her top, pushed it off her shoulders and kissed her flat belly. He reached around and unclasped her bra, letting it drop to the floor. He filled his hands with her breasts, gently kneading and suckling first one, then the other. His hands slid down to her shorts, and he removed them and her bikini panties. Standing, he lifted her in his arms and headed for the bathroom. Donovan placed her on her feet and started the water in the tub, adding some of her bubble bath. When the water was done, he carefully placed her in the tub. "Is the water too hot?"

"No, it's just right."

He placed a lingering kiss on her lips. "Enjoy your bath. I'll be back." While she took her bath, he lit candles around the room, pulled the covers back and warmed the oil he had bought in a bowl. Placing his hands on his hips, he glanced around at his handiwork and smiled.

Donovan stepped into the bathroom just as she was rising from the tub and hardened instantly at the sight of the water cascading down her glistening dark-brown skin. It had been over a week since they'd last made love, and he wanted her now. *Stick to the plan, Wright.* He picked up a fluffy towel, dried her off and wrapped it around her. Then he carried her to the bedroom and laid her in the center of the bed.

She sat up and viewed the room. "Oh, Donovan, it's… I love it!" She ran her hands over his bare chest. "You have such an amazing heart, and I'm glad it's all mine." She swirled her tongue over the spot where his heart was beating like a drum and kissed it.

"I'd hoped you would." It was the first time he had gone to such lengths for a woman. Maybe because this time, he was truly in love. He stripped the towel away and gently turned her on her stomach. Straddling her hips, he used his tongue to chart a path down the center of her spine. Donovan reached over and dipped his fingers in the oil then, starting at her shoulders, gently massaged in long strokes.

"That feels soooo good. Where did you learn to do this?"

He chuckled. "You're my test case."

"Ohhhh."

He kneaded and massaged every part of her body until she felt like putty in his hands. He rolled her onto her back, leaned down and kissed her slowly, deeply, thrusting in and out of her mouth in imitation of what he planned to do next. At length, he rose, rid himself of his shorts and underwear, and donned a condom. He kissed his way back up her body and settled between her thighs. "I love you, Simona."

He lowered his head and slid his tongue between her parted lips, capturing her tongue and absorbing her essence into his very cells. At the same time, he eased into her sweet warmth, groaning as her tight walls clamped down on him. He thrust in and out with long, deliberate strokes, going deeper each time. His hands roamed possessively over her body as he whispered tender endearments in her ear.

"Donovan. I love you, baby."

"You are my everything," he murmured.

"And you are mine."

He gasped as her feminine muscles clutched him tighter. Donovan rocked into her over and over, varying the length of his strokes, but keeping the same languid tempo. Taking his time. She arched upward and wrapped her legs around him, digging her heels into his back.

"I missed being inside of you like this. I could stay here forever."

She palmed his face and locked her gaze on his. "Then stay. Forever."

Her words broke him. He lifted her hips, threw back his head and began a hard, pounding rhythm that shook the foundation of the bed. Their ragged breathing magnified in the space, and she arched higher and met each of his driving thrusts. Their moans and cries intensified until they convulsed together. Their bodies shook and shuddered violently for an eternity as they gasped for air. He gently lowered her legs to the bed and braced himself on trembling arms. Donovan closed his eyes as the sensations continued to course through his body. He stared down at Simona's rapturous expression. "Marry me."

Her eyes popped open. "What did you say?"

"Marry me. I love you, and I want to be there for you always. I want to raise Yasmine and be there for her first day of school, when she graduates from high school and college, and to walk her down the aisle when she gets married." He placed a hand on Simona's belly. "I want to have more babies with you. To be there to wipe your forehead when you're sick, to hold your hand when we hear our baby's heartbeat for the first time and catch our son or daughter in my arms. But my greatest desire is to grow old with you. From now on, it's only you, only me."

"Oh, my God! Yes, yes, yes!" Simona threw her arms around him and cried.

He laughed as they rocked back and forth across the bed. "Okay, if you'll stop crying for a moment, I have something for you." He separated them, then reached for the box he had placed in the nightstand drawer and opened it.

Simona scooted into a sitting position and brought her hands to her mouth. "I can't believe it. It's absolutely breathtaking."

"I hope you don't mind that I found something a little different. I wanted something that exemplified your uniqueness. I've never met anyone who gives of herself the way you do." He'd had a jeweler design a two-carat princess-cut solitaire with alternating diamond and sapphire baguettes surrounding it, along with a matching band.

"No, no, no. I love it." She stuck out her hand, and he slid it into place. "Oh, my. It fits perfectly. I love you, Donovan."

"I love you, too. Only you." He drew her back down to the bed and, with a passion reserved only for her, demonstrated just how much.

Epilogue

Two years later

Donovan gazed down tenderly at his wife as he fed her ice chips and mopped her forehead with a cool towel. His life had been nothing short of amazing since marrying Simona. And they had a nice settlement from the lawsuit against Travis to top things off. While their lives had gotten back to normal, the same couldn't be said about Lorna and Travis. He hoped Travis liked his front-page notoriety as much as he did when he was spewing those lies. And if the rumors were true, the man's acting career was all but over. Good riddance.

Simona moaned. "I'm tired."

"I know, sweetheart."

"Did you check on Yasmine?"

He shook his head and smiled. She was still in caretaker mode. "Not yet. I know she's fine. Between my mom and Nana, she's probably had enough sweets to fill a Halloween bucket."

Simona started to laugh, then moaned in pain.

He held her hand, did the breathing with her and rubbed her back until the contraction passed. She had been in labor for five hours and was only four centimeters dilated. He mentally coaxed the baby to come on because he couldn't stand to see her in pain.

"Go make sure she's not on a sugar high."

It took him a moment to remember she had picked up on their previous conversation. "I don't want to leave you."

"I'll be here when you get back. Just promise to hurry."

"I promise." Donovan placed a kiss on her parched lips and turned toward the nurse.

She smiled. "It's okay. I'll take good care of Simona. She's one of our best nurses. I'll come get you if you're not back before the fun starts."

Donovan cast another worried glance Simona's way before heading to the room where his parents, Nana and her new husband, Deacon Mitchell, and Terrence waited.

"Daddy!" Yasmine jumped off her chair, ran across the room and launched herself at him.

He lifted her high and kissed her cheek. "How's Daddy's big girl?" Her greetings never failed to fill his heart with love and pride. At three years old, she already loved to read and could count to five. She would start preschool next month, and he would be there to walk her through the doors on her first day.

"Where's my baby?" she asked.

"It's not here yet."

"Why?"

"Well, sometimes it takes babies a while to get here."

"Do you have to go get it?"

"Ah, no," he answered slowly. "So, what kind of treats did Grandma and Nana bring?" he asked in an attempt to distract her. Donovan's father chuckled, and Donovan rolled his eyes.

"How's Simona, Donovan?" his mother asked.

He lowered Yasmine to the floor. "She's tired, but she insisted I come and check on this one here." He tickled Yasmine's belly, and she dissolved in a fit of laughter. "I need to check on Mommy. I'll be back in a while."

"I'll walk out with you," Terrence said. In the hallway, he placed a hand on Donovan's shoulder.

"How're you holding up?"

"About as well as you were," Donovan answered with a wry chuckle.

"That bad, huh? I survived, and so will you. As a matter of fact, I'll be back in that room in about six months."

His eyes widened. "You and Janae are having another baby? Congrats, man!"

"Yep," Terrence said proudly. "Oh, and rumor has it Karen and Damian are expecting, too."

"Hot damn! We're going to be a prolific bunch."

"No doubt. Now get in there and deliver my godson or goddaughter."

The two shared a brotherly hug, and Donovan hurried down the hall to his wife's room. "Hey, baby," he said, kissing her lips and stroking her forehead.

"Hey," she whispered. "They're not feeding Yasmine too much candy, are they?"

He chuckled. "Probably. She had about a million questions. Wanted to know why the baby's not here yet."

"Sure would've loved to hear how you answered that one," she said tiredly.

"With finesse, baby, because I got it like that."

Simona rolled her eyes and groaned.

It was another two hours before the baby's head started to emerge. "Push, sweetheart," Donovan coached.

"I am pushing. I'm too tired. I can't do this."

"Yes, you can. Come on. Hold my hand." She took hold of his hand with the next contraction, and he clenched his teeth to keep from yelling. *Where in the hell did she get this superhuman strength?* "Come on, baby," he croaked.

"All right, Dad. Now's the time," the doctor said.

Donovan moved to the other end of the bed and, following the doctor's instructions, helped deliver their baby.

"You did it, baby! We have a little boy. We have a boy," he said with all the wonder of the moment. Tears misted his eyes as he stared down at the wailing baby that would carry his name. "Hello, Donovan Elijah Wright, Jr. Welcome to the world. Let's go meet your mother." He placed the baby on Simona's belly.

"He has your eyes. He's beautiful," she cried.

"Just like his mother. I love you so much. You are my everything."

As he'd written, she was the only one who set his soul on fire. His one desire and the one he would love until the end of time.

* * * * *

REQUEST YOUR FREE BOOKS!

2 FREE NOVELS
PLUS 2 FREE GIFTS!

KIMANI ROMANCE™

Love's ultimate destination!

KROM15

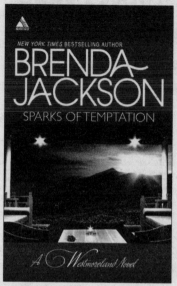